THE DROWNED DETECTIVE

THE DROWNED DETECTIVE

Neil Jordan

BLOOMSBURY

NEW YORK · LONDON · OXFORD · NEW DELHI · SYDNEY

Bloomsbury USA
An imprint of Bloomsbury Publishing Plc

1385 Broadway
New York
NY 10018
USA

50 Bedford Square
London
WC1B 3DP
UK

www.bloomsbury.com

BLOOMSBURY and the Diana logo are trademarks of Bloomsbury Publishing Plc

First published in Great Britain 2016
First U.S. edition 2016

ISBN: HB: 978-1-63286-446-8
ePub: 978-1-63286-447-5

Library of Congress Cataloguing-in-Publication Data has been applied for.

2 4 6 8 10 9 7 5 3 1

Typeset by Integra Software Services Pvt. Ltd.
Printed and bound in the U.S.A. by Berryville Graphics Inc., Berryville, Virginia

To find out more about our authors and books visit www.bloomsbury.com. Here you will find extracts, author interviews, details of forthcoming events and the option to sign up for our newsletters.

Bloomsbury books may be purchased for business or promotional use. For information on bulk purchases please contact Macmillan Corporate and Premium Sales Department at specialmarkets@macmillan.com.

For Dermot Healy
1947–2014

It was odd, I thought, as we followed the government minister in his caravan of black Mercedes four-by-fours, how often a spouse is abandoned for a less attractive alternative. This minister, for example, this ghostly presence behind tinted windows, had a wife who had hired us to trace her husband's movements, a woman whose fragrance filled the drab office we worked in, providing a welcome relief from the odour of Lynx that came from the desk beside me. She was petite, her prematurely grey hair was dyed a subtle mix of blonde and silver, she was moneyed, of course, immaculately dressed in some designer's outfit I should have known by name – Chanel, Armani, Zegna, Azzedine Alaia. They always sounded like species of rare plant, these designer names, plants I should have known. Anyway, she was clad in one of them and sat on the rickety chair and there was no denying she must have once been beautiful. She still was, by anyone's standards, a beauty that would only be accentuated by that march of tiny lines, those creases of worry round the eyelids that soon, as she explained her all-too-familiar predicament, became wet with tears. He was seeing, she believed, someone who lived in a small apartment above a neon sign that spelled out Vulcanizace, in large and vulgar letters. Vulcanisation, Frank had translated, and he seemed to share the client's distaste of the word, its implications and whatever was the process. He conversed then in his native tongue with Istvan, who generally sat in the inner room, listening for any titbits he could gauge from our increasingly tart conversations, and they repeated the word several times between themselves. Vulcanizace. Vulcan, I thought, the Roman god of fire, and I remembered those tyre-repair outfits along the Harrow Road and we eventually came to the bitter conclusion that her husband the government minister was severely compromising his security by seeing a woman who lived above a tyre-repair shop.

Istvan readied his telephoto lens and Frank guided the vehicle into the outside lane. They had a procedure, these bulked-up merchants of Mercedes 4Matic all-wheel drives, when they came to a junction. One blocked off the middle lane while the ministerial vehicle sped inside it, the others following hard at the rear. It looked impressive and sounded more so, with much screeching of tyres and blaring of outraged horns, but Frank glided the van round the whole circus quite neatly, took advantage of the chaos to execute a U-turn, and parked in a shadowed alleyway on the other side. We could see the sign from there, Vulcanizace, the three dark-windowed 4Matics mounting the pavement below it. There was a woman in the dim interior, with a large tyre in her hands. She was dressed in an old denim jumpsuit with luxuriant red hair spilling round her oil-smudged shoulders. She not only lived above the tyre shop, we realised then, she worked in it as well. And as the neatly dressed diminutive figure emerged from the ministerial car, flanked by two bulky, dark-suited minders, Istvan clicked his unblimped camera and all three of us wondered what the attraction could be.

Maybe she vulcanises him, said Frank, in his almost perfect English. Covers him in rubber.

Circus tricks, muttered Istvan.

And I remembered what fun it used to be and thought it best to leave them to it. There were issues now that diminished the enjoyment and I could see Frank's cufflinks, gleaming against the gear-handle. I remembered the tears of the attractive wife. I understood her jealousy all too well. I had a Polaroid photo in my pocket and an appointment with Gertrude. I slid back the rear door and said I was off and asked them to keep it discreet.

I knew they would. They were professionals, after all. I banged on the roof of the van as I went, a companionable goodbye, at least I hoped it sounded like one. I made my way from the alley on to the sunlit street and saw the red-headed jump-suited lover of the government minister pull down the corrugated overhead door. The sign above her flickered in useless neon in the hot glare of mid-morning. Vulcanizace.

Jealousy is unfortunately a hazard of the job. If one hasn't got it, one wants it, one wants the keen quickening of it. The way a boxer channels his anger into a random punch, I channel jealousy: I make it work for me, in a strange, disembodied, objective way. I could be jealous of a passer-by if it made the instincts work, I could be jealous of a lapdog, I could be jealous of a gnat. But the jealousy that's useful is the meditative kind, the kind that wonders what that unknown one's lunch appointment will be like, where will they sit, who will they meet, what traces will they leave. Because we all leave traces, as I had told Sarah some days ago. Some of us more than others. Like snails, silky gleaming things that follow our tracks, knowingly or not, retain bits of our residue, our memories, our fleeting pleasures, the things we have done, the things we wanted to do but hadn't got the opportunity or the time. The handbag now, that's the magpie's nest of traces, the Aladdin's cave, the Sutton Hoo of them, an archaeological hoard that someone like me could spend a good six days on. Metro tickets, supermarket receipts, loose change, sweat-hardened bills of useless currencies, scribbled notes, tubes of lipstick and the tiny white crystals that could be from a sugared sweet or a gram of cocaine.

So, while to have this teasing jealousy of what we call a randomer's life can be a good thing, to have the corrosive jealousy that infects one's own is not a good thing at all. And I tried to think of other things as I made my way towards the river. I thought of the politics of this strange place, my attempts to learn the language, and I felt twinges of all kinds of regret, about things I hadn't done or should have done or had forgotten to do. A language I had promised I would master, books I had promised myself to read, histories I should have plumbed, old enmities I should have learned about to understand this strange, fractured present. Something was about to burst, I felt, to shatter, to break, and I hoped it wasn't me. I could see the white marble towers of the parliament building gleaming above the rooftops and so I knew the river was close. I was on my way to meet Gertrude the psychic with the pet Pomeranian. *Lecturi Psihice*, her sign had read, as descriptive in its way as Vulcanizace, but far more intriguing. And it was jealousy that had drawn me to her first, that word again. I even knew it in the language. *Gelozie*. But I would visit her now in my professional capacity, nothing personal about it. Was it always part of my job, I wondered, to listen to psychics and play with Pomeranians? I had a more muscular job once, in a much hotter climate where all the enmities could be immediately understood. But that was perhaps best forgotten, like all the things I should have done.

The smell of the river was my guide, through the warren of streets that surrounded it. It was the smell of old mud, ancient unresolved politics and very current sewage. There was a barge wheeling around aimlessly in the centre, raising large concentric whorls of brown foam. Nothing is clean any more, I thought and no one will swim in that murk for a long, long time. I crossed the suspension bridge, and as I reached the last hawsers on the other side, I could see her, on the second floor of one of those by-the-river buildings. She was close to the window frame, looking down towards me with something white in her arms that could have been a cushion, a towel or even a Pomeranian. She was wearing one of those wraparound robes, a slash of yellow against the general grime.

There was a communal entrance with stairs that led to a lift, but the lift was still broken so I climbed the stairs again and wondered, would she have made coffee? Then I

5

remembered she didn't drink the stuff, as I pressed the doorbell and listened to its intermittent jingle.

I had walked with dogs in my day, before I had ended up in this forgotten place. Generally larger ones, Alsatians or Dobermans with a quick-release collar around their straining necks, a metal chain and a nightstick or a more lethal weapon that bounced off my thigh. I had even got to like them, the utterly unearned affection that they gave to me, wanting nothing in return. Large dogs were faithful, I remembered, and rarely a cause for jealousy. But I had no history with Pomeranians.

Anyway, the door now opened and the smell of old face cream met me as I entered the room and the slash of yellow that was Gertrude walked from the window and asked me to take a seat. She was drinking some green liquid from a cocktail glass through an elaborate straw. It could have been crème de menthe, it could even have been a wheatgrass smoothie, though she had never seemed to me to be the wheatgrass type. And when she spoke I detected, or maybe I imagined, a faint hint of alcohol from her breath. But she was smoking one of those electronic cigarettes as well, so it was hard to tell.

Jonathan, she said, and she pronounced my name in three separate syllables, Jo-na-than, what are we to do? stroking the feathered bundle, as if I shared her absurd attachment. Poor Phoebe has a condition that is pacific to small lapdogs.

Specific, I corrected her.

I suspect a luxating patella.

Luxating. It was odd she had no problem with that word. It made me think of enemas and bowel movements. But I was to be proved wrong.

Which means the poor dear's knee poops in and out.

Poops. I didn't bother correcting her. But I wondered about that word again. Luxating. I wondered how it sounded in her tongue.

And now she is whining – how do you say? Intermittently.

And the Pomeranian was whining, not intermittently at all, but kind of constantly.

Show me, I said, and took the little bundle in my hand. It whined as she passed it over and whined again as I fingered its knee joint under the quite ridiculous umbrella of overflowing hair.

I would take her to the vet myself, she said, but my own knees are bad today. I have trouble with the – what do you call it? Hibiscus.

Meniscus, I said. I think that's the word.

My meniscus, her patella.

And I could picture it now. The walk to the veterinarian's, with the laughable bundle in my hands, past the smoking junkies on the river and who knows what kind of witticisms thrown my way. Whatever they were I wouldn't understand them, and I was past caring.

So, she continued, and she was oddly on the ball, old Gertrude, despite her canine weakness, have you brought the photograph?

And I remembered why I had come. I had surprised myself by forgetting myself and I wondered, could I make a habit of it? It would be a sweet habit, this forgetting.

Maybe I should get a dog myself, I thought, as I took the envelope from my pocket and gently extracted the Polaroid.

Petra was crinkled and faded now. But her childlike beauty and what was the word – optimism? Hope? Lack of care, maybe. Innocence. Whatever it was, it still showed through the grimy print that had sat for too many years in her mother's handbag.

She was blonde, Petra. She was smiling, as all young girls seem to be. She was happy, I suppose. As all children are meant to be. But she had gone missing a long time ago and left her parents, called Pavel, with a residue of misery.

I should never have spoken to them, Gertrude said.

But you did, I replied. And now they'll never let go.

Remind me, she said.

Remind you of what?

What I told them.

That she was somewhere in this city.

On the east side, she said.

Yes, I said. Somewhere among those old tower blocks. A brothel, the father imagines.

Brothel? And she raised an eyebrow. I never said brothel.

She turned the old Polaroid with her painted nails.

I said a small room that she cannot leave.

2

They had come to the office four or five days ago. A country couple, on the other side of middle age, with the same lines of endurance etched on both of their faces. Their Petra had gone missing twelve years ago, in one of those resorts along the Black Sea. I had walked back into the office from a session with the therapist. Did I mention that I needed a therapist? Anyway, I had walked back into the office trying to forget the thing I couldn't forget. And he was there, Frank, and I remembered it all again. He was speaking to them in the language I was still trying to understand.

I was telling them, he said, that we do missing husbands, wives, doctored bank accounts, counterfeit vodkas and handbags. But what we don't do is missing children.

His tone of voice was neutral, matter-of-fact. He wanted them out of there, rather quickly.

There are police departments for that, I added, with a hint of what I hoped came across as solicitude in my voice.

But the mother's eyes responded. The father stared at his feet.

Police don't care, she said, in her bad English.

Police do fuck all, added the husband, spitting on the worn carpet by his ancient shoes.

And in a moment of weakness, or a moment of vengefulness – probably the latter – I took the Polaroid from Frank's cufflinked hand and saw little Petra for the first time.

Frank always wore cufflinks. They were one of those traces I was trying to forget. I had found one of them in questionable circumstances and, as he must have known about it, it would have been politic to change his habits of couture. But some habits die hard, I knew that too.

Why come to us, I asked them, after all this time?

Dream, said Mrs Pavel.

A dream? I asked.

A dream, the husband said, and he seemed weary of it all. She had a dream.

I saw her, said the wife.

You saw Petra?

Yes. She said help me. She was as pretty as the day she left.

She was a little girl, in this dream?

I lifted up the Polaroid to the light coming through the window. I heard Frank's exasperated sigh. And I must admit, it gave me some satisfaction.

My sweet little girl.

And then they went to, would you believe, a psychic, Frank muttered wearily.

He was handsome, Frank, in a kind of annoying, indeterminate way. He was ex-Special Forces, of some army that used to be. He also shaved his chest.

A psychic, I said. Mildly surprised. I had recently visited a psychic. But I would have been embarrassed to admit the reason.

Was her name Gertrude?

Gertrude, the mother said. How did you know?

Maybe because he's psychic, Frank said, wearily, and I, almost to my own surprise, found myself drawing the line at his tone.

And what did this psychic tell you?

That she's somewhere in the city. In a small room she cannot leave.

And the father spat out a word that I recognised.

Bordel.

A brothel, said Frank. He thinks she's in a brothel.

I have a daughter, I said, that age. I couldn't bear to lose her.

No? Frank said, and he gave that tight smile that I imagined Sarah knew all too well.

I wondered idly, did my daughter know it too? But she couldn't, I thought. Or maybe I hoped. That was a line that Sarah wouldn't cross.

You think they should go to the police?

I know they should.

And what will the police do?

Make a file. Stick it in a drawer. But it will be their drawer, not ours.

But I knew she would haunt me, little Petra. And we had Gertrude in common. And I would have placed any inconvenience on Frank's shoulders. This particular one seemed heaven-sent.

There are pivotal moments, I know that now. Moments where the world turns, after which everything is different. Moments where we say, later, with the benefit of hindsight, that's where it began. And they are often tinged with the shabbiest of motives. One small, recalcitrant emotion gives the world a gentle push. And that emotion was, in his language, *gelozie*.

Tell them we'll look into it, I said as my eyes moistened a little with what I hoped was a show of paternal solicitude and a sense of infinite regret.

You can't be serious.

But I can, I told him.

Why? he asked.

Because, I told him, as I held up the Polaroid, I have a daughter that age.

Her blonde hair and her hopeful eyes. The girl I knew absolutely nothing about.

Because, I told him, this face will haunt me for ever if I don't.

I waited to understand what I could of what he told them. And when the mother kissed my hand and the father stood, with ancient weariness, as if to begin a journey that should have ended long long ago, I knew he had told them rightly what I had said. And I asked him, with apparent courtesy, to make a file of the relevant details.

3

Which is how I came to be holding Phoebe the Pomeranian as Gertrude ran her fingers over the Polaroid of Petra.

Your wife, Gertrude said. You make it up with her?

Let's not talk about Sarah, I said.

But I can feel it from you, she murmured, and took a sip of her greenish liquid. Something burning inside.

What is that? I asked her. Crème de menthe?

With a mixture of wheatgrass. Quite disgusting, she said.

So, I said, you'd better tell me what you know.

You're septical, she said. I can feel it.

Sceptical, I corrected her. And I'm not, not really.

I cannot work with sceptical.

Was I sceptical about Sarah?

No, she said. You were burning. Still are. With *gelozie*. But about this little Petra, you are septic.

Sceptic, I corrected her again.

Whatever, she said. My English is bad. But if you suspend your disbelief, I can try for you.

Try what? I asked.

Map-reading, she said.

So I sat, finally, and stroked the Pomeranian's fluffed hair until the whining stopped.

You will take her to vet for me? she asked, with a hint of a smile. And she was clever, dear Gertrude.

Yes, I said. I will take her to the vet for you and suspend my disbelief if you agree to try.

Map-reading, she said again. And she laid down her cocktail glass of green stuff and unrolled a map from her dresser.

The city, she said.

I can see that.

North, south, east and west. The river between.

You said the east side.

Yes, she said, the old industrial side.

It was the new industrial side, in actuality. Or it had once been planned as new, gleaming avenues of serried concrete structures that now sat peeling, crumbling and never quite abandoned. Pools of oil-slicked mud in which children rode their bicycles, parks overgrown with ivy and weeds, the copper-coloured river flowing beneath them. But they had their own poetry, these places; the symmetry of their rectangular windows, the broken window panes and the rusting window frames retreated in a perfect perspective which promised a future that would never arrive.

And I wondered, was it that promise that had dragged me here in the first place, as she smoothed the map with her still-billowing electronic cigarette? I was a sentimentalist, a severe one. I followed instincts that I only got to understand when they were past, long past. And the clove-scented perfume of her electronic cigarette was making me queasy. I felt sick most days, but was in danger now of being nauseous.

Could you, I asked, and pushed it gently aside.

You would prefer I smoked a real one?

If you want, I said.

And of course she then did it, she lit a real one and offered another to me. I took it, again for sentimental reasons. And as the odour of real tobacco conquered the odour of fake tobacco, she sat back and smiled, the cigarette dangling from her crimson mouth.

She looked like an ageing Marlene Dietrich and she knew it. All she was missing was the eye-patch, the one Dietrich wore as she gazed through a wisp of curling smoke at the sagging hulk that was Orson Welles. They were both old then, and almost past it, and they knew it, too. And Gertrude now fluffed through her lips in that old movie way and took the Polaroid of little Petra between her old dry palms and began to rub it, as if to warm the girl who was no longer there.

In Haitian voodoo, she said, they are afraid of photographs. And you know what? They are right.

They are?

Most certainly. The chemical – what's it called?

The acetate.

The acetate. The crystals. The accretions of the light. They are jealous crystals. And they keep a little of the image they display.

You mean the soul? I asked. I was ready for anything now, even philosophical exegesis.

The crystals know something we don't. They know the face we present is just a shadow and they retain a piece of – how do you say—

The reality? I ventured.

If we can admit to such a thing.

And she rolled the Polaroid in her hands again, as if it was a tobacco leaf and she was in some Haitian basement, preparing a cigar.

And I can feel it now.

What can you feel?

The heat, she said. The real Petra.

So she may be alive, I thought. If I was to believe in this charade. And as I had promised to suspend my scepticism, I had no option but to believe. And the charade, if charade it was, had its own logic, its own rituals and its own absolute persuasiveness. It would have been hard, standing beside her, not to be convinced of something. Gertrude was, if nothing else, a convincing actress. Like that old Marlene.

Hold the map, she said, flatten it, over table.

And I did so. I smoothed all the crinkles from the old parts of the city and the once new ones. The broad snake of the river between both sides, the wide bridges over it, the grids of the grand avenues and the filigreed mazes of the little streets. I made the city flat and manageable, with my own palms, and held it down at the edges as she laid the Polaroid to one side and moved her own palm slowly over it.

Her hand was as steady as a piece of metal. And I could not help but be impressed by the rigour of it, as it moved, slowly and inexorably as a mechanical lathe, over the monochrome shapes of the city streets. If she was ever to be a junkie, I remember thinking, she would have no trouble finding a vein. Because they were raised, like pulsing iron cords, over the bone structure of her hand. The skin on the hand was pale, and I could see a hint of a red edge around the palm. Too much alcohol, I remember thinking, too much crème de menthe.

And I was engrossed in particularities like these when I caught the smell of something burning, which wasn't tobacco smoke.

It was paper.

She raised her hand a little. There was a tiny brown singed spot somewhere to the east of the river, amongst the regimental grids of the industrial suburbs. And there was a small whorl of something like smoke coming from it.

And I knew it had to be a trick and I knew it wasn't a trick, and both certainties were battling for precedence when she spoke again, softly blowing out tobacco smoke.

Somewhere here, she murmured.

Her eyes were half-closed, and the cigarette stayed between her lips and a small tumble of ash fell from it.

Down, down, down, she murmured again. And maybe she was talking about her hand, because she lowered the palm again, ever more slowly.

The curl of smoke rose from the city map. And I could smell something like paper burning.

She pulled her hand away with an involuntary gasp, and I saw the small burning hole in those city streets and put my own hand down on it, before the whole map caught fire.

There, she said.

Where? I asked.

She is there, somewhere in those buildings.

The burnt ones?

It is the map that burned, not the city.

Can you be sure? I asked.

And I could picture a portion of the city aflame now. It made as much sense as what had happened in this room did.

You try to joke, she said. Joking won't help.

So where is she? I asked.

Somewhere, she said, in those burnt streets.

A brothel? I asked.

Who said brothel? I said a small room that she cannot leave.

Sounds like a brothel to me, I said. And to her father too, I thought.

And I am done for the day, she said. With you, with Phoebe and with little Petra.

Could you do the same, I asked, on Google Maps?

No, she said. I am an analogue kind of girl. No digital for me. I will rest now, if you don't mind. You take Phoebe to the veterinarian's for her luxating patella and Gertrude will charge you nada.

Nothing?

Free. How you say? Gratis.

4

And so I walked back across the metal bridge with the map folded in my pocket and the fluffed-out Pomeranian in my arms. She whined with each step I took. Buskers looked at me and grinned. Young girls stopped to stroke her fur. The large stone angels that sat above, beside the suspension cables, seemed to have turned their heads away in silent contempt. I had a better job, I remembered again, a more urgent profession, a function even. It was to do with weaponry and rough interrogation, but that was in the old days and that war continued without me in it. I was married now, in a different city, with a daughter I loved and with a business partner who wore cufflinks.

The water below the bridge flowed with its brown lazy patterns and I suddenly remembered the colour blue. I was from a seaside home, near Penzance, where the pirates came from, and the colour blue reminded me of happiness. Blue skies, blue seas, white foam. I remembered the house, the promenade, the pier around the back of it where the swans pick their way through the mud of low tide. They looked better when the sea came in, the harbour was full, blue or fresh seagreen and glistening with reflections, each swan like a large pregnant letter S with their reflected S beneath them. I had sisters who had married, brothers who had wandered and the last of them all was my sister Dympna whose beauty was marred by a harelip that made her kind, to me in particular, and we had shared a bubble of kindness through our early days until the surgical techniques were developed that allowed her to be rid of it, so that her beauty became a fact that was acknowledged by everybody, where previously I seemed to have been its sole witness. So I had been tutored in jealousy from an early age. It was odd, to resent a vanished harelip. But it meant she was pursued then, by boyfriends, some of them even friends of mine, and our tiny shared chrysalis of emotions was shattered, though for a time neither of us could bring each other to acknowledge it. Until one day I found her in the garden shed with an older friend of mine, Peter, and got a glimpse of her beautiful thigh as his hand drew her dress above it. I'm looking for the fork, I said, since my father had asked me to dig lugworms for a night's fishing. OK, she said, and shifted her body and I could see the fork on the ground beneath the bench she was lying on. Work away, I said stupidly, as I reached for the fork, knowing I would hate Peter with a vengeance now and regretting the absence of that slash on her upper lip which had been, to me, quite beautiful. He never found her beautiful before, I remember thinking. But now that others did, he did too. And I wondered, would beauty always confuse me, in its confounding, beautiful way?

My father played the accordion with the oompah-oompah bands that drew crowds on the holidays on the bandstand on the promenade. He mended them too, which seemed to be his real job, so there were always tiny reeds laid out on the brown paper on his workbench. His workroom was off-limits to everyone but me, who liked to blow the reeds and identify their pitch and it gave him particular pleasure when I got the note right. C sharp, I would say, with the reed in my mouth, listening to the sound that was already dying, and he would say, got it in one, sailor, perfect pitch. Sailor was his word for me, and he had been a sailor once. But he belonged now to that meeting between land and sea, the eroded shore, and his house behind the harbour was right on the edge of it. He was a widower, and my mother had been for some time a dim memory. But the accordion sometimes brought her back, the wheeze and flap of it and the ripples of melody he would draw from it, the hornpipes, the polkas and the marching tunes. And occasionally one of those old laments that came from the instrument's bellows like the memory of a once beloved, exhausted breath. He grew tired in the end, my father, tired of memory, tired of life, tired of everything but me. Whatever you be, be a man, he would tell me. Because he had been a man in his time.

The memory of blue and fresh breezes. There were neither of them here, in this landlocked city, on this moulting continent, in this hot summer. And the dog in my arms was whining again, so I stroked its damaged kneecap as I walked. I left the metal bridge, passed through the stalled traffic on the other side and made my way to the address she had given me.

West or east always confused me here since I gauged them by the sea as a child and here there was only the river to divide things. West was on the right side, east on the left, facing the grotesque pile of marble that was the parliament, downriver. And I found the veterinarian's eventually, in one of those nineteenth-century courtyards on the left-hand side of things.

I had to climb a staircase to get there and found the waiting room thankfully empty, with the vet in his chamber adjacent.

Why do I know this animal? he asked.

Phoebe, I said, belongs to Gertrude.

Ah, Gertrude, he repeated. And how is she doing with the smoking?

Badly, I told him.

I cannot help her there, he murmured.

Maybe nobody can.

But to little Phoebe I can perhaps be of help.

It's her patella, I said. It is — what is the word again?

Luxating, he said and seemed to relish the vowels.

And he took the dog from my arms, to my immense relief. I felt somewhat renewed by its absence. Perhaps the rest of the day would not be so bad, perhaps all of those things I had forgotten were not of any real importance. And perhaps I might be relieved of little Phoebe and her patella problems indefinitely.

There are four grades of luxation in the patella, he told me. Grade one can be treated manually and can be popped right back in.

And he fondled the kneecap that was hidden by the mounds of fluffy hair.

Grades two to four need surgical treatment.

His fingers moved through the hair, as if testing a damaged screw.

And Phoebe, I'm saddened to tell you, is a grade four. She must rest here overnight.

I was learning more about miniature dogs and kneecaps and luxating joints than I had ever imagined. But I had other concerns. Not least the burnt hole in that map. So I thanked the veterinarian, asked him to call the clairvoyant Gertrude and explain the admittedly tragic circumstances to her.

And break the news gently, I added.

Then I went on my way.

5

She was sitting across from me in the therapist's office. She was by an open window, maybe to take advantage of the breeze from outside. And it was hot in that city, that summer. The breeze blew her hair across her cheek and reminded me of things I didn't want to be reminded of. Of an advertisement, stupidly, of a woman turning towards the viewer with brown hair blowing across her cheek, for a hair product the name of which I don't remember. It reminded me of Sarah, when I imagined she wanted to be looked at by me. It reminded me of rushes by a riverbank, an inlet near the sea, of a kingfisher darting through the rushes, the colour blue, again.

It also reminded me of that dusty, scorching room full of shell-shocked rubble where we first met. I was part of the detail to secure the wrecked museum. She was there to catalogue what was left of it. Abyssinian brooches from the first century BC. Sumerian tablets from even earlier. She was by a window then too, a ruined one that showed the burnished river and what remained of the smoking city outside. It fell to me − or did I choose the task? − to keep track of her movements and her presence there, to be the last one to leave when she did, to wait patiently in the

Mesopotamian night, sweating rivers under the flak jacket, while her small oil-lamp still burned inside among the ruins.

There is something comforting, she told me one night, driving back to the compound, in being watched.

It's my job, I told her, and of course never said what I was thinking, that I would have watched her for ever, if I was allowed.

And was it not your job, she asked, to prevent all of this ruin in the first place?

No, I said, and tried to smile, that was someone else's job.

The military's, she said, and gave a matching wry kind of smile.

Yes, I told her.

So our job, she replied, is to pick up what we can of the pieces?

No, that's your job, I said. My job is to see that you remain in one piece.

You've managed well, this far, she said.

Thank you, I told her, and was aware of boundaries already being crossed.

We had a drink that night and she told me about Eridu and Urak, the world's first cities, about Gilgamesh and Nimrod and the historical Babylon, epics of destruction that were dwarfed by the current destruction all around us. I pretended to listen and to learn, but then, as now, was just watching. The way that hair fell over her well-cut cheekbone.

And now the therapist sighed, from his seat by the bookcase, and began once more, in his tentative, heavily accented way.

So the problems have not yet resolved themselves.

You can tell?

And that was me, trying to fill the silence. I never liked long silences.

I can sense a certain . . . reluctance . . .

Please, said Sarah, and brushed the hair back from her cheekbone. But to no effect, since it slunk back again immediately. As it always had done.

You have both been under a lot of stress, lately.

Ten out of ten, she murmured.

And why is that?

Please. Isn't that your job? And isn't this shrink city?

That would be Vienna, he said, delicately.

Aren't you from Vienna? I asked, stupidly, since it was of no consequence either way.

I will admit to training there.

He obsesses, she said. About those damned cufflinks. He obsesses, constantly.

It's my job, I said, and it already sounded lame. I am employed to obsess about all sorts of things.

But about me? she asked.

Well, you are my wife, I said.

You know, I do remember that. Occasionally.

Some kind of forgiveness, said the Viennese, would be a beginning of kinds.

So, get him to say it then.

What?

That he forgives me.

For what? I asked. I have to know for what.

For whatever the fuck it is you're assuming.

He is assuming . . . some kind of intimate betrayal, the therapist murmured.

One, I said. Or many.

I won't admit to that.

Why not, Sarah?

And this was me. It would have been some kind of comfort to hear her say it, at least.

It's unmanly of you, she said. You used to be manly.

What exactly is unmanly?

This jealousy. This watching. I used to love the way he looked at me. Now I hate it.

Why?

Because it's a different kind of watching. It's obsessive. It's cold. It's unnerving.

She turned quickly, so her hair bounced around her face.

Can I smoke here?

He nodded. And she sat on the windowsill and lit one.

There's no love there. Any more. In his eyes.

And there was once?

Yes, she said, and bit her lip. Being loved by him was . . . comforting. We have a child. You know that.

Your daughter.

Jenny. And we have only fifteen minutes, doctor, before I have to pick her up.

You share a house, still.

Yes, she said, and threw the cigarette out the window.

I imagined it falling lazily to the street outside, and being trampled on by a random passer-by.

Why haven't you moved out?

Why hasn't he, doctor?

And the Viennese turned to me. His forehead formed itself into a wrinkled question mark.

It's called marriage, isn't it?

I am angry, doctor, she said. And maybe I have no right to be. But I am angry, and I don't know why.

She kissed me on the way out. On the cheek, briefly, a kiss that felt more like a smack in the face. And she left me there with him, to finish the session.

Why did you come here? he asked.

To this session? We had already paid.

No, he said, to the city.

Sarah was offered a job with the archaeological department.

The university?

Yes. And I met an ex-serviceman on an aeroplane who told me about opportunities in the former Soviet republics. I found myself a colleague, opened a tracing agency.

A tracing agency?

We find people. Who may or may not want to be found. The one who manufactures fake Glenlivet whisky. The one who markets ersatz versions of Gucci. The husband who has left his wife.

For a more attractive version?

Actually, generally less, in my experience.

And the doctor smiled.

In my experience too.

His smile thinned out, as if it hadn't meant to be there.

And your partner? Who wears the . . . he hesitated for barely a moment . . . cufflinks?

You're asking me is he a less attractive version? Of me?

No. What function does he have in the . . . scheme of things . . .

He was full of pauses, this Viennese.

He helps me on the ground. He knows the language. I put the systems in place. Or thought I would. Open another branch, in another city.

Ah. A franchise. Like Starbucks.

Yes. The Starbucks of Security. Kind of thing.

And how many branches?

Just the one, to date. Here.

Is that a concern?

No. We do well enough. Here. Just haven't . . . multiplied . . . And you're fishing now, doctor.

Fishing?

For something. What is it?

There is a lot of anger in the air.

Unjustified, you think?

I do not make judgements. I just look for the source. Frustrations in work. Disappointments in life. Can lead, of course, to stress with a marriage.

Are you asking am I disappointed in myself? Perhaps. But I love my wife, doctor. My daughter.

And she seems to love you.

Can you be sure?

I can detect a certain . . .

And here came the pause again.

. . . residual affection.

Will that be enough?

To sustain a marriage?

He shrugged.

It is better than contempt.

29

6

Contempt. I thought about the word as I made my way back towards the office. It sounded exactly like it should. Contemptuous. I should have had contempt for him, but I would have had to hate her to do that. I tried to muster it as I entered and saw him turn towards me from his computer. But I couldn't quite manage it.

You want to see? he asked. Our morning's work? Vulcanizace?

He had the file of pictures on his laptop. I leaned over his athletic, slightly bent shoulders and couldn't avoid the odour of Lynx and aftershave.

He clicked through the images. The dark shapes of the ministerial jeeps framing the lady in the oily jumpsuit, her arms around the tyre. The stooped figure of the minister, the burly minders around him. His reflective sunglasses, gleaming from the shadows as she pulled down the metal door above them.

And then? I asked him.

Then they go upstairs, he said, as he flicked on through the file.

I saw the upstairs window, the flashing red of her hair as she pulled the curtains.

We are denied the shots that could bring this shitty government down.

What shots are they?

The minister, vulcanised. Covered in rubber. A chain around his neck.

You think he's that adventurous?

You call that adventurous?

I had no answer to that one. So I returned to the safer shore of politics.

You want to do that? I asked. Bring the government down?

Somebody should, he said. Somebody will.

And I felt sorry for all three of them. Him, his vulcanising lover and his fragrant wife. They seemed players in a bad West End farce. I wished I could have felt as sorry for all three of us.

So what do we do with these? he asked.

Print them up, I said.

Istvan is already at the photo shop.

Then, send them to the client.

The wife? he asked.

She was the one who hired us.

Along with bill of charge, he said.

Of course, I said.

So I can't post them on the internet, he sighed, with a feigned kind of weariness.

No, I said. But you could open Google Maps. The east city.

He turned to me from his computer and I saw a bead of sweat on his upper lip. Which was odd, because the heat never seemed to affect him. And it was still hot, even as it grew dark outside.

Do we need to talk? he asked.

Before you open Google Maps? No.

I had contempt then. For myself. For the mundane, English bile of that statement.

He shrugged, and I had to admire the forbearance with which he did so. I unrolled the map from my pocket.

This, from Gertrude.

The psychic? You actually went to her?

Why not?

Because, it is, quite simply, insane.

Maybe I'm insane then.

No, Jonathan. You are not yet insane.

Well then. I'm getting there.

And as the same grid of streets emerged on his computer screen, I had him gradually enlarge it until it matched the exact dimensions of what Gertrude so elegantly called the analogue one.

Print it.

He stuck a cable in his laptop and pressed Print.

I placed the burnt map over the fresh one, and drew a circle round the small burnt hole.

Somewhere among those streets, there is a brothel. How do you say it?

Bordel. How do you know?

I can only assume.

And can we now talk?

About what? I asked him.

About cufflinks, he said.

No, I told him.

And I looked at the loose button on his shirt. His chest, as I noticed for the umpteenth time, was shaved.

Some other time.

7

It was dark when I walked out. There was a soft summer rain falling. It brought a smell of dust to the air that was almost sweet. I thought I might walk home, all of the way; forty minutes or so it would take me, and if the rain kept up there would not be too much damage. To my jacket, my hair. The damp felt welcome, after the day's heat. Over the river, up those small ascending streets towards the hills. Jenny would be playing with her dolls in the hallway, always the hallway, for some reason. I would cook, or Sarah would, or wonder of wonders, we both might, and find a way to soften whatever had happened between us. They say a marriage is never truly a marriage until it has dealt with an infidelity. And if that was so, perhaps we were well on our way to being married.

I was on the bridge then, walking alone for once over the brown river, and I stopped to look at one of the carved angels with their immobile feathered stone wings that seemed designed to keep watch over those waters. I twisted the gold band off my finger and looked through it at the currents beneath. There was the circular frame, soft and out of focus, and the dark passage of the river, one enclosing the other. Was that what a marriage was to the vicissitudes of life, I wondered, something barely noticed yet comforting that enclosed all of the chaos in gold. I heard a cough above me then, or a sob, and I turned, too quickly, because the ring slipped from my fingers and fell, slowly it seemed, tumbling over and over, into the brown river below. I remember wondering, would Sarah notice? And if she ever did, when would that day be?

I heard the cough again, but it was more like a choked, suppressed gurgle and I thought of someone drowning. Maybe my ring, drifting and absolutely lost now, towards the mud of the riverbed. Then I saw a shadow by the foot of the stone angel, huddled beneath its glistening, motionless wing. The shadow moved a little, and it was a woman, squatting or crouching there. She was young. Young enough to make me think of suicide and all of the attractions of oblivion. If she wanted to jump it was her choice, I reasoned, but I already knew that reason doesn't come into such things. So I spoke one word, loud enough that she could hear.

Don't, I said.

Don't what? she asked, without turning. And I could tell that her English was good. And I was already climbing up beside her.

Don't jump, I said.

Why would I jump? she asked.

I don't know, I said. Why would anybody?

Maybe to know, she said, what it feels like.

She had her head still turned from me. And I edged closer, round the great stone wing of the statue.

The architect jumped, I've been told.

Why do you say that? she asked.

I'm not sure, I said.

Just to keep talking, she said. You think if you keep talking, I won't.

You won't jump?

And it wasn't the architect. It was the sculptor of the angels.

Why did he jump?

Because of the eyes.

What eyes?

When the bridge was finished, he realised he'd forgotten to carve out the eyes. So he jumped.

And I said something stupid then, just to keep the conversation going.

So those angels are eyeless?

She said, yes. Blind. Cannot watch over the river.

And she turned to me. Long lashes blinked over a pair of brown eyes.

Stupid historical fact.

And she jumped.

I saw her body fall, in a long straight plumb line to the darkened waters. And I noticed the most irrelevant of details. She had coloured canvas sandals. And something about them made me jump too.

I hit the water as if I was cracking a sheet of ice. And then there was brown, foaming, oily liquid flooding my nostrils, from them to the roof of my mouth. I would have vomited, if I could have. I could see nothing but darkness, probably kept my eyes closed, so would have been no help if she was floundering beside me, and then some instinct took over and I swam up towards the surface. I saw a slicked head, bobbing up beside me like a seal, but it was a girl and she was gasping for breath, so I gripped her beneath her armpits and managed to say, Just let me do this. And I swam with her, towards the west side.

She lay against me like a dead weight and I thought I saw a smile on her face.

Kick your legs, I said, if you can.

And I saw those coloured sandals break the surface of the brown foam. So we made our way, together, towards the sloping bank of concrete.

There was the detritus of a great river there, waterlogged pieces of wood, rusted bedsprings, tin cans, old shoes. And I laid her like a piece of flotsam on the concrete bank.

Why you do that? she asked.

Why did I do it, I corrected her. And I honestly don't know.

If you don't know, what about me?

You're alive, at least.

You think?

And I threw up then, whatever liquid I had swallowed. The bile slid down the weedy bank, back towards the river.

You need help, she said.

And I almost laughed.

I do?

You need to drink fresh water, dry your clothes.

And what about you?

Me too, she said. Both of us.

Where?

Anywhere.

And she stood. She was like a drowned cat, with dank river mud in her dark hair.

You need a hospital, I said.

You think a hospital would help?

Help what? I wondered. Whatever urge made her take that leap? Whatever urge made me take it too? And then the question seemed absurd.

No, it probably wouldn't help.

We could stand in the emergency place. For hours until we dry. Ask for hairdryer, maybe.

I can't just leave you here, I told her.

No?

You might jump again.

From here?

And she looked down at the river. The brown, uninviting foam. There shouldn't have been foam, but then the water shouldn't have been brown, either.

What if I didn't jump? What if I slipped?

Even so, I said. I still can't leave you here.

So then, she stood. Take me to hospital. Outpatients. You know where it is?

No, I admitted.

Of course you don't. I will have to lead you there.

Where is it?

Twenty minutes' walk. Five minutes' taxi. You could also take me home.

Where is home?

A few blocks away.

Blocks. The Americanism sounded odd in her accent. I would have said streets. But she turned then, and walked towards the nearest steps without looking back. And it seemed natural, inevitable, even, that I should follow.

There were metal steps leading through a stone tunnel to the street, with intermittent, fast-driving traffic. And when we crossed the road, she took my damp arm.

You're wet, she said.

No more than you.

But I don't wear a suit. You . . . you squish . . .

And I did. I could hear the water ooze from my damp shoes with every step.

Did you save me? she asked.

I wondered. Would she have swum to the other shore, without my help? Would she have even jumped, without my presence there? It was an act that needed to be observed for its dramatic potency. She only jumped to be seen jumping, in the knowledge that she could be saved. And I thought of a riddle I would ask my sister before they cured her harelip, by the promenade and the blue blue sea. What would you rather be, nearly drowned or nearly saved?

Would you have swum to the other shore, I asked her, if nobody was there?

No, she said, as we sidestepped an oncoming pair of headlights and reached the pavement on the other side.

Not the east side.

Why not the east side? I asked.

Because, she said, and, with a gentle touch on my elbow, led me towards the next set of steps, it is not my side.

So, I had saved her. And we both seemed to accept that as we walked past the whores and their pimps who stood in twos and threes in the summer night. I had saved her and her presence on my arm seemed testament to that fact. And I noticed for the first time that the rain had stopped.

Does it come with a responsibility? I wanted to ask her, do I have to validate somehow the life you would have finished? But the question seemed absurd, and I didn't even know how to ask it. She was alive, and who knows what would have happened had I not been there.

You had better tell me why, I said to her. Why you did the thing you did . . . or wanted to do . . .

And again the question was half-formed, but somehow she understood.

She stopped over a metal grating outside the back of a hotel and the wind from below lifted her skirt.

I think you know, she said.

And I did know. There is only one reason for that urge. Somebody hurt you.

Hush, she said. That's enough.

She took two steps backwards and leant her head into the underground breeze. It was like a giant dryer now, lifting her dark hair into a perfect fan.

Stand here, she said, with me.

Why?

You are wet, like me. Dry your clothes.

I walked three or four steps over, so my dripping shoes stood beside her canvas plimsolls. The warm air ran up my legs, making ridiculous balloons out of my trousers.

Open out your shirt.

She pulled at the parts of my shirt that were still tucked in my belt.

My shirt ballooned and I held it out, so even the sleeves filled with the warm air.

Turn, she said.

And she turned. Her dress filled out like a flower, and the dark pistil of her hair seemed to surge upwards, as if it was being pulled from above.

The giant blow-dryer, she said, of the river god.

There is a river god?

Yes, she said. And if you ever get wet again, remember that his blow-dryer is here.

She took my arm then, and led me off the grating, towards a small alley beyond.

Home, she said. I remember. Just a few blocks away.

Blocks. That Americanism again. And it seemed particularly inappropriate for the streets she led me through, small cobbled places, with arches every now and then, that led into communal courtyards.

She stopped by one particular arch and I remember it had decorative tiles, halfway up the walls, covering the ceiling.

Come, she said.

And, as always, the courtyard seemed larger and more fanciful than the arch outside would have intimated.

Come up, she said, and began to ascend one of those circular stone stairways.

I followed again. There was a gleam of yellow light as a curtain was pulled in an adjacent apartment. An older woman stared, behind the reflective glass. And the wet girl turned her head, as if she didn't want to be seen.

She felt for a handle in the dark, and found it locked.

Keys, I said.

Yes, she said. I had keys.

And she opened the old wooden door and walked inside as if she expected me to follow. And I did.

Hello home, she said in the darkness. And as she closed the door on her peering neighbour, Goodbye Mrs.

We stood in the darkness then, before she fumbled for the light.

I remember you.

And the light came on and as my eyes grew accustomed to it I saw one of those crumbling interiors, again larger than the door outside might have intimated. High, unpainted walls, and a patchy ceiling with the cornices falling off. There was an old sofa with a cello lying on it.

She walked to the sofa and plucked one of the cello strings. The note echoed and lost itself amongst the old plasterwork above.

You're a musician? I asked.

I was, she said. Once.

Can I use the bathroom? I asked.

Over there, she said, and nodded her head.

I walked towards the door she had indicated and closed it behind me. There was a small basin with a cracked mirror above it. I washed my hands under the tap and some sandy residue flowed off them into the plughole. I heard the cello sound from inside, a series of notes from long ago. Something by Bach, I imagined, though music wasn't my speciality. I washed the mud of the river off my face then and looked at my face in the misted mirror. There was a dark blue robe hanging from a nail in the wall beside me. It was a man's robe, and it seemed to have its own story, hanging there. I turned from the mirror and dried my face in the old fabric and inhaled the odour of someone else. Male, undoubtedly. And I wondered was he the one who drove her to that place on the bridge. He was vain, whoever he was, I remember thinking, because the towelly fabric smelt heavily of cheap hair oil.

8

When I left she was playing the same notes from long ago that flowed around her like a slow river. I asked her what the piece was and I had a sad frisson of satisfaction when she told me it was Bach, one of his cello suites. I asked would she be all right and she nodded and when I said goodbye she nodded again and never paused in her playing. There was nothing left to say, although it seemed there was something I should have said, but whatever it was, I couldn't think of it. So I traced my way back down the steps and saw the woman in the adjacent apartment pull back her lace curtain again.

Goodbye Mrs, I said, echoing her phrase, and the steps led me to the courtyard where the arch framed the traffic passing by outside. I hailed a taxi and I was already halfway to our suburban home before I realised I had never asked her name.

A small faux-rustic two-storeyed home in a winding street. It had fake wooden beams embedded in the concrete walls and something Tyrolean about the roof, chimneys that looked like miniature turrets. It could have been in the Austrian Alps or the Pyrenees, but it wasn't, it was here and we had rented it and it had been home for the past several years. There was a sad garden of trees, laurel, linden or willow, I had never bothered to find out which, though they left a bed of yellow pods and shrivelled flowers in the springtime, so they may have been willows. Somebody had built it, if not with love, at least with obsessive attention to fanciful detail. There was a wooden gate carved with something like hunting horns, or they could have been meerschaum pipes with strange gargoylish faces round what may have been intended as pipe-bowls. However many times I swung it open, I never worked it out. There was a name for them, maybe in some Mitteleuropean encyclopedia, but let me for the moment describe them as grimly fantastical and oppressively strange. It always creaked when I opened it and sometimes Jenny was alert enough inside to hear the creak and run to the door so that when I was turning my key in the lock she already had it open. But this didn't happen, that evening.

I walked down the small gravelled pathway and put my key in the lock. I turned the key slowly and when the door swung open I saw Jenny sitting in the beam of light that came from the kitchen, her dolls arrayed around her on the parquet floor.

It's Daddy, Jessica, and he's late again.

Sorry, my love, I said, as I closed the door behind me and trod my way quietly down the hall towards her.

And his feet are wet, she said. How observant of her, I thought. She gave names to her dolls that I could never remember, and to her ever-widening variety of imaginary friends.

And now you're stepping on Melanie's dress.

Say sorry to Melanie for me.

I stepped sideways and left a footprint on the empty floor.

She heard you. But now her dress is all yucky.

Oh dear. I shifted my feet sideways again.

And now you're on Rebecca's toe.

So there was a Rebecca as well, I thought. She was a new addition. I jumped sideways again.

And when did Rebecca join us?

Oh, I forget. She just turned up, sort of.

Sorry, Rebecca.

Apology accepted.

Rebecca doesn't hold grudges?

No. She's not the grudgy type. But if you walk all over her again she may not come back. Then what will Melanie do?

She'll have you to play with, I said. I did a slow kind of shuffle towards her, without crushing any more imaginary limbs. Then I reached down and lifted her towards me.

She needs more friends than me.

Why would anyone need more than you?

She likes a crowd around her. At all times.

A little like my Jenny then.

I kissed her where the curls of her hair met her neck. She twisted and giggled.

Maybe.

If she hasn't got enough friends, she can always invent them.

Maybe so, she repeated.

It's a wonderful ability, I said. Means you'll never be lonely.

And she looked lonely for a moment, unbearably lonely, and I was sorry I had mentioned the word. So I brought up another word, equally loaded.

Where's Mummy?

She's cooking dinner.

Maybe she needs a hand?

And I edged into the kitchen with her, and only then became aware of it. The sound of a cello.

Maybe it had only started then. Or maybe I had only then become aware of it.

Sarah was sitting at the bare wooden table, reading by the light of the table lamp, while an array of pots bubbled behind her. And the music was coming from the CD unit on the wall.

What's that? I asked her.

Some kind of curry.

No, I meant the music.

Oh. That's Pablo Casals. The cello suites. I found them in an old suitcase. They were still wrapped.

A present from somebody?

Must have been.

Not from me.

You would have remembered, surely. Or I would have.

She looked up, eyes peering above her reading glasses. She seemed like the academic Sarah again, and I liked that.

I'm reading about them now.

Mmmm?

I moved around the kitchen and kissed the top of her head. And wonder of wonders, she allowed me to do it. And we stayed like that, three heads bowed together for a moment or so while the cello, rich and dark as treacle, filled the room.

He revived them.

Who? I asked.

Casals. They were regarded as nothing more than training exercises until he recorded them in the 1940s. And now they're regarded as – she quoted from the sleeve notes she was holding – 'the pinnacle of musical perfection'.

Wow.

Yes. Wow. And shall we have some curry now?

Let me do it, I said, and set Jenny on the floor, who immediately clambered up on her mother's knee.

Daddy's shoes are all wet.

Are they?

Yes, I lied to her. It was raining for a bit. Must have stepped in a puddle.

And I wondered why I was lying. Or was I even lying? It had been raining and I could well have stepped in a puddle. But the truth seemed too complicated to relate at this juncture, and the events earlier that evening seemed as remote as a dream.

There were three bowls: one with rice, one with chicken bubbling in a curry sauce and one with steaming vegetables. I laid out three plates and did my best with the ladle.

Daddy's messy, Jenny observed.

Yes, darling. Daddies generally are.

And we ate then, in silence for a while, with the cello winding its spell around us, until Jenny asked could we turn it off.

You don't like it?

It's not me, she said. Melanie thinks it's too sad.

And I got a quick glance from Sarah, who disapproved of imaginary friends. She considered them a pale substitute for real friends, of which Jenny had all too few.

Melanie doesn't take violin lessons. Jenny does.

You could learn from this, darling, Sarah said. He was a legendary cellist.

Cellist, Jenny repeated, between mouthfuls.

It is good? I asked. I felt the need to change the subject. And after dinner, bedtime, I said.

Mmm, she nodded, and her eyes were already half-closed. She seemed too tired to eat.

Have I had enough? she asked.

One more mouthful, Sarah said. Then Daddy will take you to bed.

OK.

And she opened her mouth the way children do and stuffed it with the largest spoonful she could manage, so the curry sauce dribbled from her closed lips down towards her chin.

Yuck, said Sarah. Table manners.

Gnnrnrym, said Jenny. Or something without vowels anyway. Her mouth was so full, she couldn't have managed them.

I lifted her, as her cheeks worked away.

Kiss Mummy goodnight.

49

When you've wiped your mouth.

So I grabbed a handtowel and wiped it clean, and brought her puckered lips down towards Sarah's.

Yuck, said Sarah. And double yuck.

I told her a story as I tucked her into bed. About Johnny McGory will I begin it; that's all that's in it. She laughed again, as expected, and asked for a real one. So I made one up, about an imaginary friend and a real friend who swapped places every now and then. The imaginary friend was left-handed and the real friend was right-handed. They had identical dolls, the real and imaginary, and identical families and were identical in every respect except for the hands with which they played their violins. The imaginary friend played her bow with the right hand, the real friend played hers with the left hand. And it didn't really matter, since in the imaginary world left was right and right was left, a mirror image of the real one. It only became a problem when they had to practise violin. Dreadful amateur screechings ensued where once there had been just a beautiful tune. And I was at my wits' end as to how to conclude this story when I heard her breathing turn into a low soft snore and saw that her eyes were closed. So I pulled the cover over her and tiptoed back to the kitchen.

Do we have to talk about it all? Sarah asked. And when I shook my head, she took the cork out of a bottle of wine and poured two glasses.

But I still can't believe you went to that psychic.

Why not? I asked. The jealous mind will do anything.

Is that a quote? she asked. From a security handbook?

No. But you went to a therapist.

Didn't we say we wouldn't talk about it? she murmured, and took a sip of wine.

You started.

I know, she said, and she gripped my hand. She almost crushed the fingers together. Please.

Tell me something then.

You want me to tell you that I love you?

That would be refreshing, I said.

How? she asked. Since you must know that.

She drank more wine.

We found a girl, in a bog.

A corpse?

It looked like a squashed leather bag. Early Bronze period. The skull was crushed. The throat was cut. Either a murder, or some kind of ritual killing.

So it happened even then.

What happened?

Abduction. Rape. Murder.

We're talking about a pre-pastoral society. She smiled. They did things differently then.

So you can't blame the jealous husband?

The nipples were cut off. There were symmetrical slashes round the torso. Some ritual we don't know of yet was involved. Or—

Maybe a serial killer with a nipple obsession.

It was all about you, you know. Not him.

And it was a sudden shift, this, from the Bronze Age nippleless shrivelled body in a bog.

Was it?

Yes. You were away. I needed someone to talk to. I had my own Jonathan obsession.

Ah.

I wanted to get your office done before you came back.

Please.

Well. You don't want to hear. I understand.

She brought my hand to her shirt. She was wearing no bra. I could feel her nipple underneath the cloth.

Maybe she cut them off. As some kind of penance.

The girl in the bog?

Not really a girl. She's more like a pressed piece of leather now. Or a sculpture by one of those post-modern whatsits.

Conceptual artists?

Yes. Whatever they call themselves.

She was a little drunk. And the cello, from some kind of allegro movement, had gone into a more contemplative mode. It sounded like thick, syrupy brown bog water. I thought of the leathery girl with her nipples cut off. And I felt Sarah's nipple harden under the cloth.

What do you think, she asked, could we try again?

Is that what we call it now? Trying?

For a long time we didn't need a name for it. But maybe now we do. The thing we did without thinking needs to be thought about.

And talked about, too?

Maybe.

Isn't that what the therapist is for? Talking about it.

Oh God, she said, Jonathan, please.

I'm sorry.

You're always sorry. And so am I. And maybe that's where we live now. In the land of sorry.

Sorrow?

No. I said sorry. One is sorry. One acts sorry. One makes up. Sorrow is different. Sorrow is a state, like depression. And I'm going to bed.

She stood up, swaying slightly.

You can come if you want. You can stay if you want, and finish that bottle. But that's where I'll be.

And I sat there, listening to the brown, syrupy music for a while. I thought of the jumping girl, and I wondered what her name was. I thought of little Petra in the small room that she couldn't leave. I thought of Jenny's imaginary friends. And I realised that all of this thinking was a way of forgetting about the thing that couldn't be thought about. And with that thought I followed Sarah to the bedroom.

She was already asleep. I crept in silently beside her and curled up my body the way hers was curled, close but not close enough to touch. She was wearing those short flowered knickers she always wore and she still had the body for it, like a youngish girl. She shifted a little in her sleep and moved her buttocks automatically towards me and I didn't move, towards her or away. It felt like a memory of something more than a promise of something. And I must have fallen asleep.

9

I was woken by the sound of falling water. I wondered, was it the sound of rain? I turned my head slowly and saw the curtains drawn on the French windows and the sun hitting the garden trees and I realised Sarah was having a shower. The clear glass of the bathroom door was mottled with steam and there was a blurred female shape standing in the bath beyond it. There was too much glass in this house, I remember thinking. All of the alpine promise of the exterior, the gate, the roof, the chimney, was not carried through into an interior of mottled glass, plastic curtains, false marble tables and once-clear Perspex. But she was there, behind two layers of steamed surfaces, like a pointillist nude painted by whom? Odilon Redon, maybe. She came through then, wrapped in a towel, and smiled at me, as she began assembling her clothes for the day. She slipped thin underwear on with a lace floral rim and wrapped an athletic brassière round her thin breasts in one of those deft movements that once stopped my heart. How did women do it? I wondered. The arms crooked round the shoulder-blades and the hands clasping the unseen clip. She dipped her head and massaged her dangling hair with the towel and smiled at me again, upside down this time, and asked me would I be taking Jenny to school.

I would like that, I said.

Well, you'd better get a move on then, she said, and struggled into a summery dress and stepped into two canvas slip-on shoes. I've a lecture at nine.

So I began to get a move on. I angled my legs out of the bed on to the floor and she came towards me and bent her head down so that her hair was all around my face.

You smell musty, she said.

Bad? I asked her.

No. Just kind of musty. Take a shower. I'll wake Jenny on my way out.

And she brought her lips towards me and moved her head this way and that so they brushed off mine. It was more a nuzzle than a kiss, but it felt more than fine. We were shy when we first met, so our hands and lips would touch without our eyes really meeting, and it reminded me of that. Our lovemaking had been urgent and immediate, but rarely discussed. We didn't need to discuss it and we didn't know then it was a paradise that would be hard to return to.

I had a quick shower, dried my hair, pulled my clothes on, listening to the sounds of plates and cutlery clinking from the kitchen inside. And only when I heard the sounds of goodbyes and the front door slam did I finish the charade. I walked out into the hallway and realised, with a large dollop of shame, that I had been waiting until Sarah had left. Jenny was playing idly with the star-shaped cereal in her bowl. She was fully dressed and had her hair twisted into a ponytail.

Hey there, sweetie, I said and palmed the hair on the top of her head.

You're taking me to school? she asked.

That seems to be the case, I told her.

Why don't you both do it?

Because, I said, parents lead busy lives.

Busy busy busy, she answered, as if addressing some fundamental fact about life in the twenty-first century.

But there was peace in that kitchen, even if it was the peace of absence. I poured myself juice, boiled the kettle, made us both some toast and realised I had traversed the floor several times without stepping on imaginary presences. Maybe they lived busy lives too, I surmised. And I was wondering what life would be like with just the two of us when she, with uncanny precision, voiced my thoughts.

Is Mummy going to leave you?

Why would you think that? I asked. And I immediately knew why she would think it.

Because she says you don't look at her any more.

I never tire of looking at her.

So why does she think you don't?

Don't what?

Look at her.

You're not making sense, Jenny.

I know. That's what Mummy said. Sometimes things stop making sense.

She played a little more with the soggy star-shaped cereal. The pastel colours were all merging into a pink soup.

And if she does leave you, will I go with her or stay with you?

That's not going to happen, darling.

Melanie thinks I should go with her. But then Jessica thinks I should stay with you.

So they were back, and performing some therapeutic function for her. Cheaper than our Viennese, I thought.

You shouldn't listen to imaginary friends.

I don't have real ones to talk to.

You have, I tried to reassure her. You have plenty of friends in school. And we had better hurry now, or we'll be late.

She returned to the theme as we sat in a traffic jam, approaching one of the bridges over the river.

It's not as if my friends don't talk, but they speak English funny.

She was at the Lycée International, with children of diplomats, businessmen and various bourgeois transients. And she had many friends; I could see it every time I dropped her off, when they crowded round her like some exotic specimen.

So you prefer imaginary ones?

Only ones I can understand.

And I decided to leave it at that. The traffic finally shifted, and I pulled in by the little faded park across from the municipal exterior. It had been a government building once, with art deco columns, decorative brickwork and with muscular versions of an ideal proletariat carved on the door. But it now housed the Lycée.

I kissed her and told her I would pick her up at three.

For music, she said. I forgot my case.

But I didn't, I said. I had it perched in the passenger seat beside me. It'll be waiting here.

And she ran, then, with a sudden outburst of childlike enthusiasm and was soon surrounded by a flock of real, chattering friends on the broad, churchlike steps.

IO

Pussy Riot, said Frank. Coming this way.

I remembered the whip-wielding Cossacks at the Sochi Olympics, the business inside the Moscow church, the girls in coloured balaclavas playing fake guitars.

Not the originals, he said. Kind of cover version.

We were walking through a market in the burnt-out cathedral, the immense ruined nave of which enclosed an endless bazaar of improvised stalls. He had stopped by one stall selling balaclavas coloured in playful pink, yellow, blue, every pastel shade of the spectrum.

They're selling like hot cakes.

Who buys them? I asked.

Kids, he said, who want to imitate the pussy aesthetic.

Which is?

You must know. That punk S&M LGBT whatever.

We passed another stall, selling black balaclavas and ex-army fatigues.

Patriots and Russophiles, they wear the black.

But we're not chasing coloured balaclavas.

No, he said. We are chasing the fake Gucci.

He walked on through that ruined cathedral of stalls. He struck gold then, behind a huge hexagonal stone pillar. Bags, of every designer variety, on display.

I fingered a pink calfskin one with an elegant bamboo-type handle. With Made In Italy embossed in a half-circle beneath the zip, above the Gucci logo.

Two hundred, said the kid behind the counter. Good present for your lady.

Why so much? I asked him.

Why you think? he said. Genuine Gucci.

Give you a hundred, I told him. Though why I was bargaining, I had no idea.

One seventy-five.

One fifty.

OK, one fifty. Cash.

And so I counted out the notes. I took the unwrapped bag and we walked on.

Perfect copy.

There's a little piece of Italy just outside Tbilisi.

So we have to go to Georgia?

No, I said. Someone else can do that. We send this bag to Gucci. Send them a bill.

We left the market by the rear of the cathedral with its broken flying buttresses and I could see the river flowing by again behind the small, ruined graveyard.

What is it about this place? I asked him. They do things the old-fashioned way. They fall in love, they kiss in metros, they hire detectives to follow errant spouses and psychics to find lost children.

You could call it retro, he said.

Maybe it's something to do with communism?

But that's all gone now.

Like in a horror movie. The ghost always comes back.

We should talk, he said.

Isn't that what we're doing? Talking.

I mean have a drink, talk.

Like the old days? No.

Look, I know there's—

You know I know you were teaching my wife the language.

She doesn't need lessons.

I'm going to have to let you go.

There was a long silence. He moved from one foot to the other on the grass.

When did you decide that?

Just now. We've done the Gucci thing. And I'm letting you go.

Does it feel good, saying it?

Actually it does. Clear out the desk. The situation is untenable, wouldn't you agree?

He said nothing. He leaned against a yew tree and adjusted his cuffs. He stared straight ahead at the flowing river, the cufflinks showing underneath his jacket. He always wore a jacket, whatever the heat. The cufflinks were star-shaped today, with the tiny glint of what probably was a fake diamond. He must have had several pairs. His handsome face showed no emotion, and there was a certain dignity in the way he didn't throw even a whisper of a glance towards me. I felt a sudden rush of a feeling that I didn't fully understand. Guilt, maybe, shame at a basic lack of human courtesy. The situation may have been untenable, but perhaps it deserved more conversation. Even the condemned man is given the opportunity to explain. But I felt an unruly freedom as well, as I left him there and walked through the broken graves towards the roadway and the river.

Some kind of bird screeched to my left, a gull, maybe, but we were so far from the sea, how could a gull be possible? I kept walking, knowing I should leave the office empty for the afternoon, giving him time enough to clear out his things without further embarrassment. And the bridge then loomed up before me, with the giant blind angels guarding the river below. I turned right and walked across it and felt a fresh wind from the water underneath and wondered once again, was it time to leave this place and return to blue sea and salt sea breezes? And as I reached the other side I heard the sound of music through the grind of gears and the sounds of the crawling vehicles. Maybe there was a radio playing from an open window, and I became aware of one, the tub thump of some kind of hip hop from a car window through which a woman dangled a hand with a lit cigarette. I walked on and all I could hear was music now, a cacophony of clashing worlds coming from each traffic-jammed car. I crossed between the bumpers to get to the other side, and walked up the stone steps underneath the metal arch and found myself on the promenade by the cheap hotels and tourist restaurants where the hookers strolled by night. And it was crowded too, with young backpackers and agile pensioners with walking sticks, so I turned into the warren of streets beyond and heard music again and recognised the sound of a cello, rich and dark. I walked underneath a cement passageway and found myself in one of those old courtyards, which I didn't recognise at first. But the cello sounded from somewhere above, languorous and familiar. And I crossed the courtyard and found the same stone steps and realised I was at the building that she had led me to last night, but that I had approached it from the other side.

But it was the same, without a doubt, the decorative tiling above the arch and the open grilled gate leading to the quiet street outside. The traffic was nothing but a distant murmur and seemed to be there just to create a bed of sound over which the cello could soar. It was another one of those Bach suites and I made a mental note to familiarise myself with them, so I could recognise one from the other. There were six of them in all, I remembered from the booklet with the Casals CD, each with a prelude, a saraband, a gigue and whatever else they called that succession of baroque dances. I wondered if Jenny could learn them one day; could they be transposed to the child's violin she played? And I began climbing the stairs, following the resonant sound, and when I saw the same woman's face staring at me through the lace-curtain windows, I knew I was back at her door.

I stood there for a while, feeling those eyes behind the glass on me. Then I heard the sound of a curtain pulled, and I placed one finger on the door.

It was unlocked and it opened with a slow creak of wood. The cello came through, richer and fuller. It was as if whomever was playing it had hit a more intense vein of emotion. Or maybe the door had been impeding the sound. It swung open, wide enough for me to walk through. And she was there on the sofa, the broad wooden shape between her knees, drawing on the bow.

She allowed the bow to scrape to a slow halt when she saw me. The residual sound echoed round her like a broken promise.

Hello, she said.

You remember me?

I remember. You came to see was I still OK?

No. I found myself on the street outside. I heard the music playing. I followed it up.

I was practising. The cello suites.

Which one was that?

The second. In D minor.

You're a musician?

I would hope so.

I mean a professional?

I was. I'm on sabbatical, from the opera.

The state opera?

Is there another one?

They had them in every breakaway republic. The roads might be in ruins, the streetlamps barely flickering, one could set one's watch to the blackouts, but somewhere, on a once-elegant street, the state opera still functioned. Generally a late-twenties façade of constructivist concrete and marble, or, in this case, a fin-de-siècle wedding-cake architectural fantasy, with broad steps and carved granite caryatids and fractured orchestral flurries drifting from it in the daylight hours. I had passed it many times with hardly a thought.

You like opera?

Hush, she said. If you want to stay here, hush and let me finish.

So I walked past her and the sofa to the window. I saw the street outside that we had walked down, wet and in last night's darkness. Was it really last night? It seemed months ago, suddenly. The pavement was cut in half by sunlight, a boy led a thin horse down it, pulling a cart loaded with abandoned tyres. His head was blunt and dark and he could have pulled the same horse two or three decades ago. And maybe it was the music that placed the street outside time, because she was finishing now, with two held chords that seemed to clutch the hours between their fingers. And then she released them and the sound was gone.

Is that the end? I asked.

Of the prelude, she said.

Oh, so there will be more. And I waited for time to do its trick again.

There's an allemande, courante, saraband, minuet. No, wait, two minuets.

I waited for her to start again, but she didn't.

My wife, I said, played them for me last night.

You have a wife? Of course you do.

Why of course?

Because I saw the ring, falling into the water.

I rubbed my finger and thumb around the bone of my third left-hand finger. It felt naked without it.

She plays this thing too?

And I smiled. That would have been the strangest trick of all.

No. She played a CD. What's his name. Pablo Casals.

You came here to talk about your wife?

No. I came here quite by accident.

A happy accident.

You think?

She leaned her head towards my hand, as if she needed something to rest on. She was tired, I thought, and my hand accepted the weight of her head. I brought my other hand to the other side of her face, but her hair was falling backwards, so it touched her cheek.

Enough of that, she said. Let me practise.

You want me to go? I asked.

Stay as long as you want. But I have to play.

She brought her lips briefly to my finger. For a moment I thought she might bite it.

Sit over there. Close your eyes.

Won't I distract you?

No, she said. You remind me that I'm alive.

II

Alive, I thought, it's what we all want to feel, as I descended the stairs, one or maybe two hours later. Alive meant time was a fluid river, so that a minute could last one hour, and an hour one minute. The curtain was pulled once more, to hide a dark, watching face. The courtyard with its cobbled surface seemed to rise to meet me and the metal balconies seemed to circle above, with their creeping, late-afternoon shadows. I walked back the way I had come, through the small stone archway, and there was no cello playing. And there was something else I was trying to forget now; it was to do with a blunt-heeled shoe and the instep of the foot beneath it, it was to do with the whisper of released clothing against skin, textures of linen and silk and the dust wheeling in the bands of sunlight coming through the window, above the sad mattress. It was a sad mattress, spread out on a frayed carpet of the floor of what you could hardly call a bedroom. There was the cello, perched on the sofa like an observant cat, and I imagined I was inside that cello, looking through one of the S's cut into the wood at the open doorway and the broad beam of sunlight in the room beyond, above the mattress and the two bodies twisting in some kind of combat on it. It was a slow, luxurious kind of combat with the untwining of a limb or the rise and fall of a flank signifying capture or surrender. There were no winners, only losers in this field of flesh and muscle, and so I knew I should forget it, or remember it for ever. So I did my best to forget.

Forgetting meant walking, so I walked again. Through the small backstreets to one of the wide promenades that led to the river, and the yawning bridge above it. Two oriental tourists asked me to help with their photograph and so I held their camera and obeyed their instructions about what to include in the frame. Angels, they said, angels. So I took two steps backwards and tilted the camera upwards so that two of the statues above the parapet loomed above their smiling faces.

Do you know those angels are blind? I asked them as I showed them the digital image. They nodded with approval and thanks but with no understanding.

Stupid historical fact, I said, and handed the camera back.

And I nodded and smiled, and bowed and continued on my way to the other side.

Istvan was alone in the office and was wondering why that was the case. He was holding the map of the city with the burnt hole in it. He was wondering why that was the case too.

I had to let Frank go, I said.

Ferenc? he asked, and I nodded.

Should I ask why? he asked.

You already have, I said, and no, you shouldn't.

I could tell, he said delicately, that things weren't what they should have been.

You noticed a certain tension? I asked.

It is my job, he said, to notice things.

And this map, he said, with the burnt hole somewhere in the twelfth district . . .

Is it the twelfth?

It was the first time I'd become aware of that.

The twelfth, he said, with a small singed fraction of the fifteenth. Our city once had Parisian pretensions. Based on the Napoleonic arrondissements.

Did Napoleon get this far? I asked. And I was so intent on forgetting, I would have sat through a history tutorial.

Napoleon the Third, he said, not Bonaparte. And the Grande Armée never made it here. It passed to the west, on its way towards Moscow.

Istvan was plump, with an owlish face and a kind demeanour. What he most enjoyed was never getting to the point.

You have burnt a hole with your cigarette, maybe? When lacking a ballpoint pen?

I don't smoke.

Ah. So the map burnt itself?

In a manner of speaking.

You are speaking in tongues.

His mention of biblical tongues made me think of angels. Eyeless and blind to the river below them.

You remember the parents? I said. Searching for their missing daughter?

You insisted we engage with them.

They went to a psychic. And the psychic did some business with that map.

She burnt it with her cigarette?

How did you know it was a she?

I remember the conversation. I was listening, in the other room.

Of course, he would have been. And it was his job, after all. I began to look forward, now, to life in these offices with just the two of us.

Gertrude. She claims the girl, Petra, is in a small room that she cannot leave. Somewhere in the burnt section of that map.

A brothel. In the environs of the twelfth and the fifteenth.

If they are the burnt bits.

They are, believe me.

All burnt now, and smoking. I imagined laser-guided missiles, broken buildings, charred bodies.

How long to find out?, I asked him.

There are brothels everywhere. But in the twelfth, the fifteenth? It depends on their status.

You mean legality?

They are all quasi-legal. I mean, how much above the radar. What they offer. If it is girls, under-age . . .

If it is?

It will take more time. And I pity the parents.

She went missing years ago.

Ah. On the legal end of things then, perhaps. And I still pity the parents. Maybe even more. All those years, and not knowing.

He folded the burnt map, carefully.

Give me three, four days . . .

You have it, I said.

Is this a punishment duty, he asked, or an enticement to a partnership?

A bit of both, perhaps. There's only two of us now.

Yes. Two.

12

I was walking past a bookshop on the main boulevard
when I saw a bowed head I recognised, behind the reflections of the passing traffic. I walked inside and it was her,
Sarah, fingering some paperback with her face towards the
shelves. I could take time there to see what a picture she
made and to comprehend how any random passer-by might
admire her, and possibly desire her. She seemed untouched
by the heat, wearing the same light summer dress that she
had left the house in, and I moved closer, and tried to pretend
to myself she was a stranger. Her weight was on her left foot
and the canvas sandal with the raised heel was hanging loose
on the right. The thin muscular calf and the ankle, swinging
lazily back and forwards, with the sandal making the slightest of sounds on the wooden floor. And I was almost behind
her, inhaling her scent, when she turned and looked at me
without any surprise whatsoever. She grimaced, then smiled.

Are you checking on me? she asked.

Yes, I told her. I'm an obsessive-compulsive wife-checker.

And you're funny, for once.

I'm on my way to pick up Jenny, I said. It's her music
time. And what's your excuse?

I'm on a break, she said, between lectures.

She thumbed the book then, and for the first time I noticed her nails. They were varnished, red.

New nails, I said.

Yes, she said. There's a place that does them round the corner.

She thumbed the book again.

It's called *Nine Suitcases*. About a couple who got stuck in a city like this, during the war. Because the wife wouldn't travel without her nine suitcases. They ended up in separate camps. But they survived.

Separately or together?

I'd have to buy it to find out.

She turned her head to the book, and I moved my face near to the nape of her neck. I inhaled her hair, and felt how different it was, how real. It almost had a taste, like vanilla. And she said, without turning round, I want to be with you when we're older, Jonathan. When we get through all of this.

I let him go, I said.

Oh God, she said.

Wasn't the situation kind of untenable?

Maybe, she said.

We both thought so, I lied. And I wondered why I was lying.

And maybe you're right. It's just so . . .

So what?

So obvious. So vulgar. Unmanly.

And there was that word again. I had to do something about it.

You used to be strong, my dear, she said.

Isn't a sacking better than a throttling?

Are you so sure?

I'm sure.

Yes. You're sure about everything, now. Aren't you? She turned and looked at me and there were tears in her eyes. And we're not through it yet.

No?

No. We're in a plane. Over some strange city. In a holding pattern.

She looked at her watch.

And doesn't one of us have to pick up Jenny?

Me, I said. I have her music in the car.

Go on then.

And her hand reached out and squeezed mine, briefly. I turned it and saw again the newly painted nails.

I envy women, I said.

Why?

These strange rituals, all this beauty stuff.

I brought the red nails to my lips.

Gives us time to think, she said. I could paint yours sometime.

Or would that be too unmanly?

13

She was waiting for me on the broad steps with her schoolbag between her tiny ankles.

You're late, she said, and I told her I was sorry and lifted her and placed her in the passenger seat.

My violin, she asked, and I told her it was in the boot. So she opened her music as we drove and practised with her fingers on an invisible finger-board. She functioned very well, I thought, among imaginary things, holding her chin down as if on an actual violin, her fingers moving across small, non-existent strings. I crossed the river again as she played and quietly hummed and hit traffic on the other side, so I parked in a side street and began to walk.

Why this way? she asked.

Because of the traffic, I told her.

You'll get lost, she said.

No, I told her, I know these backstreets.

And I was beginning to. The shadowed arches, each of which held a courtyard with the sagging balconies and the curving steps. And I heard it again, dim, but unmistakable, from several roofs across, the sound of a distant cello.

Someone's practising, she said.

Yes, I said, a cellist.

You can hear it? she asked, and I remember thinking it was odd.

Yes, I said, why shouldn't I?

Because, she said, I'm not sure everyone can.

And the sound had faded now, or we had walked too far beyond it, and a group of schoolgirls came running down the cobbles, their laughter filling the air.

They can't hear it.

Because it's stopped.

No, she said, listen.

And we both stopped and listened. But I heard nothing.

Cellist, she said. Sounds like jealous.

She moved her hand again on the invisible strings, and hummed. And she kept humming till we came to the avenue with the alfresco tables and the bored waiters and the music college beyond, with the sounds of fractured practising coming from every open window.

I waited while she walked up the steps into the great black hole behind the open door. I could hear flutes echoing from the building above, pianos, double basses, what seemed like a fractured orchestra, but no more sound of cello.

There was a small graveyard behind it. I had made it my habit to wander there while I waited out her lesson. The angled slabs with their incomprehensible names, the ivy creeping over the stone angel and the broken statue of some forgotten hero of a forgotten resistance.

I sat on a bench and my telephone rang and I saw Frank's name come up, so I left it unanswered. Then I saw, beyond two lanes of graves across from me, a couple sitting in the shade of an old yew tree. The woman, plump and broad-hipped, had spread a napkin out between them and was paring a rind of cheese on to slices of bread. The man was pouring coffee from a flask. And I recognised the Pavels, husband and wife. They seemed out of place in the distant hum of traffic that was the city, lonely, yet intimately connected. And I walked towards them, wondering was that what the future held for all of us.

I have forgotten your name, the husband said, with a country-peasant formality.

Jonathan, I told him.

I would offer you coffee, but we have only one cup.

I'm fine.

Is this ... accident ... or did you search us out?

My daughter, I said, takes violin lessons in the academy.

The wife chewed at the rind of cheese, as if anxious to waste none of it.

So, you have no news?

My partner's searching, I told him, a grid of streets around the twelfth district.

You trust psychic?

No, I said. It's borderline unprofessional. But you do.

So, we should wait?

Haven't you waited twelve years?

I mean in the city. We were wondering whether to return home.

Where is home?

He mentioned a village with a kind of blunt contempt.

Is it far from here?

Two hours by train.

You should go home then. Any news and we can contact you.

We can stare at the same walls. Walk the same streets.

What is it like, the waiting?

She prays. Every day. I listen.

You don't pray?

And he almost smiled, showing blackened teeth. He spat in the dust by his leather shoes. As I turned to go, the woman's voice stopped me.

Thank you, she said.

For what? I've got no news yet.

For believing.

14

The cufflink came first. Lying in her purse, like some kind of memento. One shouldn't look into purses, or if one does, one should swallow the consequences. But the purse and the handbag are the burial mounds of the trade, hidden hoards that just beg to be excavated. And surveillance becomes a habit of kinds, the watchful eye, the gaze that once looked with a kind of voluptuous fondness becomes gradually colder, more observant. It was there one morning and the next morning was gone. She had returned it, I supposed, and I tried to think no more of it. But at his desk he had a habit of fixing them before he picked up the phone, took up his pen, and what kind of man was it that wore immaculate shirts in the summer heat, shirts with silver baubles on the cuffs? I couldn't avoid that glint of silver when he shook my hand, which he did often, in that thumb-grasping half-American kind of way, when he turned the car wheel, when he adjusted his necktie. A fog descended, a jealous fog, and I confused it with the summer heat haze, the mist that emanated from the humidifiers of the street cafés. And I passed that sign one day that read 'psychic readings' in both languages and took those most irrational steps, up the stairs by the broken lift, and first made the acquaintance of Gertrude and her Pomeranian. She read my palm and predicted nothing but she knew how to soothe the soul somehow, in that old-fashioned Middle European way. She had a voice that sounded like it emerged from a coal-tar pit with an infinite sense of ennui that knew that everything passes, even jealousy and bile. So I allowed myself to forget it, that little gleaming question mark of silver, until I found the hotel charge on her Visa bill. And then of course I had to visit it, a brutalist concrete pile along the river front, with shabbily dressed business-men coming and going and well-dressed ladies sitting in the lounges. I questioned the room-service charge and was given a printout of the bill, complete with the costs of cable TV and miniature vodka bottles from the mini-bar, five of them.

I know you want me to explain, she told me, but I can't. You were away so much, I was redesigning the office, I was choosing those adjustable swivel-backed chairs that would have helped with your posture. The things a wife thinks about, how her husband stands, what he eats, how he dresses, is he happy, has his eye wandered, do those trips to other cities mean something other than business, is he taking more care of his health, does he drink too much coffee, and more to the point is that feeling we engen-dered together in the Mesopotamian heat still there, like the oily Euphrates, flowing between us towards the burn-ing Arabian sea. Does he still care for me, am I still attractive, have I put on too much weight since the birth, is there too much room in that space between my legs where I used to love holding you still and tight until the urgency took over. All of those things that I can't explain, couldn't talk about, I began to talk through with him and yes, he would adjust his cufflinks as he listened and keep his calm inscrutable face in the listening mode and he was handsome, you know that, but without those eyes that I could sink into for ever, without that mouth that crinkled downwards; he was nothing like you. And yes, I met him for a drink in that drab concrete hotel and did I have some intent? I can't be sure, but I hired a babysitter for the night and hired a room and paid for it because with him you always paid. And I drank too much, champagne and wine at first then those small vodka bottles, and many many cigarettes – I was eating them that night, out of nervousness, out of need; you were away of course and we began by talking about you and finished by talking about you. And please don't ask me about what happened in between, I'm shy about those things and eaten up with guilt, the guilt that came down on me like a sudden cloud when I woke on my own in that tousled bed and saw his cufflink glittering on the faux-woollen carpet. It stank, that carpet, of male feet and sour wine and vomit. I washed myself in that plastic coffin they called a shower but couldn't wash myself clean and maybe I never will. And I picked up that cufflink and put it in my purse to give it back to him and maybe that was the real mistake, because that's where you found it.

15

I was tossing a salad in the kitchen and Jenny was practising her violin in the living room when I heard three sombre notes, followed by six or seven rapid ones. And Sarah turned to me and asked me when she had learned them.

I took her to music today, remember?

But that's Bach, she said, from the cello suites.

You sure?

I played them yesterday, from the Casals CD.

She hears everything, I said.

And the playing stopped now and Jenny appeared in the doorway.

Where did you learn that? Sarah asked.

From the cellist, she said.

What cellist?

On the way to music. She was playing.

You heard a street musician?

I couldn't see her. Only heard her.

And you worked out how to play it?

I can hear it, she said. So can Jessica.

Ah. Your imaginary friend.

Yes, she said. She's helping me to learn.

And she moved her fingers over an invisible neck.

Do you think it's healthy, she asked, as we lay in the midnight heat on the bed without covers, these imaginary friends?

Maybe she should see the therapist too, I murmured.

Stop it, she said, and moved her body towards me. I could feel the perspiration on my stomach meeting hers.

Can't we just get back to loving each other?

We can try, I said.

I never stopped, she said. During, before or after.

Enough, I said, and I put my arms around her and the slow thing began.

Come on, she said, come on, you can do better than that.

Certainly, I said, and it was like the old times for a while, familiar and easeful, and she gave a long and satisfied sigh.

I bought the book, she said.

What book? I asked.

The book about the nine suitcases. I read about how they made it through. They were in separate camps. They tried to stop loving each other. It would have made it easier. But they didn't succeed.

So they failed too.

Yes. They couldn't stop. Can we stop, do you think?

Shall we try?

I'm not sure, she said, and placed her nose in my armpit.

You smell different.

But she didn't. She smelt just like she always did, in the heat, after the event.

16

Taste it, she said.

She held the decorative glass towards me, full of the green liquid.

Wheatgrass, she said.

No alcohol?

Too early for that. I could make you coffee, but I don't drink the stuff.

There was a tiny scraping of heels from the kitchen and in walked the Pomeranian. She had a splint of some kind attached to her back leg. Her white hair flowered over the top of it, like some exotic plant.

How is the patella?

He is an excellent vetinarian.

Veterinarian, I corrected her.

Whatever, as they say. The joint is back in place.

And the dog limped towards me and stood staring at my ankles. I didn't dare pick her up.

I've forgotten her name.

Jonathan, Jonathan, how could you? Her name is Phoebe.

Phoebe, I repeated, and bent down and tried to stroke that profusion of hair. But she took several tiny toy-like steps backwards.

So, to what do I owe the privilege?

My wife, I told her, still says she loves me.

I am *psyckai*, not therapist, Jonathan.

But you're a good listener. And you know certain things.

Yes, I can tell, she said. There's something dying inside you.

Dying?

Or something dead. Something has died. Present or past tense, I do not know.

You do not deal in tenses?

No, time is fluid with these things.

Ah. You deal in multiple timelines. Like a multiverse.

Don't be clinical, Jonathan.

You meant to say cynical.

So I did. But there has been a meeting, and something has died. All I can tell.

In me?

Your marriage? Is it dead? Dying?

I hope not.

And you have therapist for that. Therapists deal with dead and dying marriages. I deal simply with the dead.

Can we talk of something else? I asked her.

Please. Because, we keep talking this way, I must charge.

I don't mind paying, I said, but please talk of something else.

Are you that lonely, Jonathan? Is impossible, with that mouth of yours. It would have been my type of mouth, many years ago. When I had a type.

And I could well imagine. Gertrude, with some Sven or Alix, beautiful enough then to drive them quite insane. The cigarette dangling from her painted lip. And she took up an electronic version of it now, clouded herself in a puff of pungent smoke.

The little girl, Petra, she asked, have you found her yet?

My colleague, I said, and it felt odd saying that. What was Istvan anyway? Associate? Employee? Prevaricator? Anyway, he had plodded the twelfth district and found something.

Your colleague?

Istvan. Has found out there is a brothel, on several floors of one of those old apartment complexes.

So there is a reason for your coming here?

Yes.

But I never said brothel.

You said a small room she cannot leave. Which sounds like a brothel to me.

I pressed some buttons on my phone and brought a picture up. Of a fifties apartment block in an identikit row. A broken concrete path leading to it, with windows reflecting the evening sun. They gleamed, like so many blind-man's eyes.

And how can I help?

I don't know. How can you?

I need things I can touch.

I took out the Polaroid again from my pocket. Little Petra smiled at us both with all of the innocence of her ten years. Gertrude placed it between her palms and did her strange thing. Which consisted of her half-closing her painted eyelids and gritting her teeth together with an odd half-smile. Not quite a trance, I remember thinking. More of a meditation.

You are close to her, she said. And she opened those blue eyes.

A good detective.

You're saying she's here?

I'm saying you're close. No more, no less. And for that, you must pay me. No receipts.

17

The sound this time was like a summons, authoritative and plangent at once. I was standing by a café, trying to get whatever relief I could from the spray of the mist dispenser, when I heard it, carried on a wave of heat maybe, the same thermal that blew the mist towards my face. A series of descending notes to the lowest string, then a matching ascent with just a hint of melody in the progression. Here we go again, I thought, someone's calling me, and perhaps my act of forgetting had been too effective, because I began walking towards the source without forming an image of who it was. And the progression kept going, as if the notes obeyed some sweet mathematical algorithm that didn't want to end. I know now it was the prelude to the third cello suite – in time I would get to hear all of them, and that she practised them in sequence. Life begins and ends with Bach, she would tell me, and there turned out to be more truth to that than I could ever have imagined. But for the moment I just followed the sound. I would lose it traversing a bank of houses, then turn down another street and there it would be again. And I found myself at the entrance this time, with the river of sound flooding the arch with its tiled ceilings, tracing its arabesque round the balconies inside. And I walked, of course, up the steps, towards the open door and she was inside, playing, in a white summer dress appropriate to the heat of the day.

Hello again, she said without breaking the stride of her bow. Have you come to tell me something?

What could I tell you? I asked.

I don't know, she said. Something. About why you're here.

Because I heard you play.

About what you do.

You want to know what I do?

And she must have come to the end of the prelude then, because she lifted her bow.

I find people, I said.

Ah, she said. Like a detective.

Sort of, I said.

You must be a good one then.

Why do you say that?

Because you found me.

And she returned the bow to the strings and I wondered was it the shadow of the instrument between her legs, then realised it couldn't be. There was something staining her dress, spreading from where she wrapped the cello between her legs, and it was red. Blood. She was bleeding, and didn't know it.

You're bleeding, I said.

What? she asked, and her eyes were half-closed as she was lost again in her playing.

You're bleeding. Badly.

I moved towards her, touched the dress around her calf and raised my finger, soaked with blood.

I know, she said.

Don't move.

I won't. Let me play.

You need a hospital.

I don't, she said. It's what happens.

What?

After you lose a child. Bleeding.

Has it happened before?

Yes.

Stop playing.

I can't. I won't. Music is the only thing that helps.

That's insane. You'll damage yourself.

I'm already damaged.

Is that why you were on the bridge?

Yes. You brought me back. So I'm yours now.

What does that mean?

But I already knew, somewhere inside me. I had cheated her out of what she wanted. She was alive now, and the fault was mine.

And she stopped her bow.

Help me up, she said.

I took the cello from between her legs and rested it on the sofa. I put my hand beneath her armpit and brought her to her feet. She laid her head against mine then, with an infinite weariness, and I felt the nausea of sudden panic. I needed to get out of there, but didn't know how.

The shower, she said. Let me take a shower.

I helped her towards it, and once in the bathroom, she raised her hands towards the ceiling, like a little girl.

Pull the dress off.

I did that and she stood there, almost naked but for a pair of cotton knickers that were half red, half white.

You could rinse it, she said, in cold water, while I shower.

She stepped inside the shower unit and the water came down the sad mottled glass, gradually steaming it, obscuring the shape of her body and the ripples of pink it left.

You can go if you like, she said.

I was filling the basin with cold water. I rolled her dress in it, kneading it, so the blood spread out through the water like printer's ink.

I can't just leave you here.

Yes, you can. I'm all right now. I expected this.

And I was desperate to go just then. I felt I was drowning, in someone else's life.

Can I check on you again?

To see if I'm all right? Yes, you must. Just tell me one thing.

There was the barest outline now, of a naked body behind the misted glass. The voice carried over the hissing steam.

What?

Are we to be friends, or lovers?

What kind of question is that?

Friends help each other. Lovers hurt each other.

Is that the rule?

Generally.

I dried my hands on the only towel there. I began walking very quietly towards the door. For some reason I didn't want her to hear me going.

Can we be both?

I turned, and there she was. Standing in the wettened dress. Like a drowned thing again, and the cloth that had been white had a soft, drenched patina of pink to it.

Both? I asked, rather stupidly.

Yes. Both would be good. For a change.

You put the dress back on, I said.

Yes, she said.

I had just rinsed it.

It's hot, she said, too hot. I can't play in this heat.

But she sat, back on the sofa, and began plucking at the cello strings.

And you want to go now. Yes, she said, I understand. But you must answer, before you go. Can we be both?

Perhaps, I said.

Ah. Only perhaps.

She raised her wet face to me and presented a brave smile.

You want to think about it, don't you?

Perhaps I do.

So. Think about it. And you must kiss me before you go.

18

So I kissed her before I left. I took her small chin between my fingers and raised those broad, wet lips to mine. I felt a rapid, darting tongue come between them, searching for my own. And I promised to check in on her again. Though as I walked back down the stone steps, as her neighbour glanced at me behind her lace curtain, as the cello sounded out again behind her door, I knew I wouldn't, or shouldn't. Some things are just too strange. They should be left in the realm of possibility, or imagination. I had pulled her from the river, yes. I had helped her home. But the thought of some ultimate responsibility, some promise, like the promise of her tongue, darting between her lips, was too much, much too much. I felt I couldn't breathe, in that heat; I felt I was suddenly drowning in warm water. And there was a man standing on the pavement beyond the archway, dressed in a dark linen suit. How do they wear suits in this heat? I remember thinking.

You hear that music?

I had passed him before he spoke. So I had to turn to see if he had spoken to me.

Do I hear that music?

It was almost lost, out here on the street.

Yes, I hear it. Barely.

So it is not only me.

No. I hear it.

And a distant phrase came to its end. There was silence from inside the courtyard, the rattle of distant children's voices.

And now it's stopped.

Now you don't hear it?

No, I said, I don't. How could I, when it has stopped?

Don't you find the phrasing is too – *erzelmi*?

Erzelmi? I knew the word.

Emotional.

Aha. A critic, I thought.

Should music not be emotional?

Good question, he said, and turned on his heel and walked away.

It was to be a day like that. A day of abrupt transitions, of non sequiturs, of arbitrary connections. I walked behind him until the cobbled street ended in a broader one, a boulevard, and I wondered at the fact that he never looked around. Shiny patent-leather shoes on the hot cobblestones, which could have sweated in that heat.

There was traffic held on the boulevard, a demonstration of some kind. Groups of men in haphazard military fatigues blocking the traffic island, arms punching the hot air, an incomprehensible slogan echoing. Lines of police in flak jackets, guard dogs on leashes.

I would have followed him out of a sense of idle curiosity, if nothing else, but he was soon lost in the crush of bodies. And Istvan, when I finally made it to the office, was sitting in the breeze of the desk fan, cleaning a weapon in his hand with a handkerchief.

You need that? I asked him.

It was a Makarov double-action, and I had cleared him a licence for it.

You hear that noise out there?

I passed the demo.

Well, he said. I might, some day.

And what's the issue now? I asked him.

Balaclavas, he said.

Balaclavas?

We have our own Pussy Rioters. A demonstration. Which means they jump up and down with fake guitars and coloured balaclavas. Then some patriot punks put on black balaclavas to throw rocks at them. Police pretend to keep the peace. We will all kill each other soon.

Dare I ask why?

Doesn't matter why. We are – how you say it? – a kind of blanket.

You mean a patchwork quilt?

Right first time. Patchwork quilt, with thread fraying. The black balaclava kills the coloured one, which might bring out the kefiah and the burkah that maybe kills them all.

How soon?

Doesn't matter how soon. What matters is to be ready.

He cocked the weapon and pointed it through the open window at the street outside.

Pop, he said.

That easy? I asked him.

Sadly, yes.

Put it away now.

And he returned the gun to its drawer beneath his desk.

I called the brothel. In the twelfth arrondissement.

And?

I asked for a Petra. They smelt – how do you call it? A mole?

A rat, I offered.

Correct. Smelt a rat. Put down the phone. So there's only one way to check now. Pose as client.

You?

Hardly me. They know my type.

How?

I have Special Forces written all over me.

You don't mean me?

Why not? British businessman. Alone in foreign city. What could be more natural?

Or unnatural.

As you wish. Ask for a blonde. Twenty years or so. Say a Petra was recommended.

By who?

Does it matter? A colleague. Any travelling scumbag. Maybe you meet her. In the small room that she cannot leave. Case closed, as they say on cable series.

19

Was mid-afternoon the time for sex? I wondered. Certain kinds, maybe. I parked the car by a small canal and looked from the image on my phone to the line of apartment blocks across the way. They looked different of course, without the sun reflected from the windows, less sinister, different yet the same. I had called, to ask for a girl. There was a long pause, and the sound of the telephone being set down, then lifted, and a woman's voice replaced the man who had answered. Her English was refined, with a slight theatrical gravitas to it. Who recommended us? she asked. A colleague, I told her, from London. Mr Samuelson. And you? she asked. From London too, I told her. Mr Baker. Samuelson, she repeated. He recommended a girl called Petra, blonde, in her early twenties. Petra, she repeated. Yes, Petra is quite special. In some demand. We run a clean establishment. No funny business. And you, sir, do not demand funny business. And I wondered then what funny business entailed. But I assured her I wanted none of it.

And as I crossed the road, walked down the broken pavement towards the building, the sun must have dropped a notch or two, because the upper-storey windows began to blaze it back towards me, like silvered reflective sunglasses. Was there something sinister in their apparent gaze, or was it my imagination? It was the latter, I persuaded myself. And I was a London businessman on a routine visit to a quite ordinary brothel.

There was a rusty metal lift with a mother wheeling a buggy from it and, once inside, the acrid odour of urine. I pressed the button for the third floor, and, somewhat absurdly, turned up my collar, hoping no one else got in on the way up.

It whined upwards, stopped at two empty floors and I saw two dim corridors stretch away from the doors, towards pools of afternoon sunlight. And the third floor was identical to the first and the second, down to the shaft of sunlight at the end.

I stepped from the lift and the doors closed behind me. There were four doors to my left and four to my right, and a broken window to the end of them, with a pigeon standing in the metal frame.

A door opened then, and the pigeon took to the air. A man stood there, playing with the zip on the top of his tracksuit.

Mr Baker? he said.

Yes, I said.

You pay cash, he said. And yes, I had it ready. I reached for my inside pocket and he shook his head.

Not here, he said. Inside.

He nudged the door open with his foot, and I walked in.

There were soft chintzy curtains covering the windows, dampening the hard daylight. There was a tailor's dummy sitting incongruously to one side, her plaster face frozen in a smile, one hand held upwards that seemed to be waiting for a non-existent teacup. There was a sofa against the wall with a glass-topped table in front of it and I took a seat there, as the door closed softly behind me. There was a small bell sitting on the table, and I had no idea what its purpose was. Then I heard the door closing softly behind me, and I realised I had entered alone.

I sat there for an unbearable five minutes or so, inhaling the odour of old cigarette smoke, and eventually, out of exasperation, I rang the bell.

Be with you, a woman's voice answered, and I recognised the anglicised tones coming from behind the door to my left. It was a room of doors, three of them: two of them facing each other and one facing the muted light from the window. And I wondered, did the establishment, as she had insisted on calling it on the phone, extend the length of the whole corridor outside? And then the door to my left opened and she was there.

A capacious lady in a pink tracksuit, dark hair piled into a kind of nest on the top of her small head.

Mr Baker, she said. I'm Maria.

Maria, I said and rose and held out my hand before I realised the gesture was unnecessary and unwanted. I assumed the name was as fictional as my own.

From London, she said, and took my hand, ever so briefly.

Staying at the Radisson?

Yes, I lied again.

And you were recommended my Petra?

I nodded and she smiled, stiffly.

She is a special girl, she said, a little bit shy maybe but Englishmen like them shy.

You know England? I asked.

Mayfair, Windsor, Royal Ascot. Brighton.

Margate, I added, hoping to fill out the list.

Bath, Southend-on-Sea.

I had only ever known it as Southend. But I nodded, appreciatively.

Lyme Regis.

Had she been a tourist guide? I wondered.

Where they shot movie – you remember—

The French Lieutenant's Woman.

Meryl Streep and my favourite—

Jeremy Irons?

Yes. Now, to the money business—

You've been to all those places? I asked idly, as I took the rolled bundle from my pocket.

Been to, read about. And Petra price, three hundred.

How long has Petra been –

In this establishment? Not long. She is shy girl, you will see. And her fingers whipped through the notes, with alarming expertise.

Two hours, condoms by the bedside. No funny business.

I nodded, some shabby understanding. There would be no funny business.

Hove, she said. Hastings.

Harrow, I replied. This list seemed to substitute for conversation.

Harrow-on-the-Hill, she corrected me.

Of course, I said. Harrow-on-the-Hill. She held open the door and I walked through and found another door facing me.

Inside, she said. And she held up two fingers.

I opened the door.

Blackpool, she said, as it closed behind me.

20

She was sitting with her back to me, in a salmon-coloured negligée that exposed her thin arms. Her hair was cut like a blonde pageboy's and there were dark roots showing at the parting on the scalp.

There was a bed, and a bathroom with a toilet bowl and bidet and a door that must have opened into another bedroom beyond.

Petra, I asked, and she said, yes, that's my name and somehow I immediately knew it wasn't.

I walked towards her and she lay back on the pink coverlet with the small fluffy pieces of cloth and I stupidly wondered what they called such a bedspread and the word candlewick came to me. So she lay back on the candlewick bedspread. Her face was waiting to be kissed and it was thin and there were lines around her lips and the soft dull bruising on her arms that the make-up couldn't quite hide.

How old are you, Petra? I asked.

Nineteen, she said.

And how long have you been here?

Oh, she said, I come and go.

Her face was waiting for the kiss, and when she felt it wasn't coming, she flipped over on the bed and began to fumble with my belt.

Don't, I said.

You wanted Petra, she said.

But you're not her.

How can you tell?

Because you're not nineteen.

And the lines around her sweet mouth deepened.

Was nineteen once.

I'm sure.

Is Petra nineteen?

She would be in her early twenties.

What does it matter what my name is? You want Petra, I'll be Petra.

It matters, I said, because a girl named Petra went missing many years ago.

Then you just pretend she was me. I went missing.

Do you live here?

No one lives here but Madame. This is a place for fuck. You want to fuck?

No, I said, but it's important you tell me. How many girls are here?

They come and go, she said. Four or five. What are you, cop? I don't want no trouble.

You won't get it, I promise. Tell me their names.

You don't want to fuck, you must be cop. There is no Petra, I promise. And if you don't want to fuck, let me jerk you off at least.

Her hand reached once more for my belt and I grabbed it.

Anya, Anya, Anya, Anya. Anya's my name. You promise you're not cop?

I'm not, I said.

You just want to talk?

I just want to talk.

You mind then if I do my thing?

What thing?

My drug thing?

I shook my head, and touched the bruises on the inside of her arm.

While we talk. Talk for an hour, then you leave, tell Madame you had good time. You promise?

She opened the bedside-table drawer and took a pouch from it. She took a cigarette packet from the pouch.

You mind if I smoke?

I shook my head.

Bad for you, smoking. Not like fucking.

She took a spoon from the pouch, a needle, a rubber medical band.

She lit the cigarette and did the business while it dangled from her lip.

You leave now, you cause me trouble. Don't want to fuck, I understand. Just don't leave now.

She was as dexterous as a medic with her works, and I found the spectacle compulsive. Numbingly compulsive. She heated the spoon with the cigarette lighter while the ash fell from her mouth. She filled the needle from a table-side glass, squirted it clear into the air, then drew the liquid from the heated spoon. She wrapped the rubber round her arm and whacked her vein into action.

Hold this, she said, and gave me one end of the rubber tube.

I saw the needle penetrate the make-up over her vein. A small cloud of blood puffed into the syringe before she hit it home. Then she sighed, a long exhausted sigh, and her head fell backwards against the bedboard.

Petra, she said, and closed her eyes and there was a long silence.

After an age her eyelids opened. Two pinned black pupils stared at me.

Tell me about Petra.

And so I told her. I told her everything. Something about those tiny pupils made it necessary. About the psychic and the burning map. About the girl I had pulled from the water. About the Bach cello suites. About Jenny's imaginary friends. About the lost Petra and the brothel in the twelfth.

Here, she said. The twelfth.

Yes, I said.

But, she said, there's something you're not telling me.

And there was. There was the cufflink, the hotel bill, the therapist, the half-saved marriage. So I told her all of that too.

You are lost, she said.

Yes, I told her, quite lost.

And Petra, she is lost too.

She smiled, softly.

And you, I said. You need help.

I wish I was her, she said. Because I am lost as well. But if I was her, at least I would have been found.

*　　*　　*

Windsor, said the madam as I walked back out.

Yes, I said. Sandringham.

Balmoral, she said. All the royal places.

Kensington Palace.

You liked Petra? she asked. And maybe she had tired of the British place names.

Yes, I said. Very much.

You come back, she said. A good client is rare.

I fly back to England tomorrow.

Ah, she said. Salford.

No, I said. London.

London, she said.

21

Her list of place names had made me long for home. Southend-on-Sea. Harrow-on-the-Hill. Salford, to which I'd never been. London. I followed the road along the canal, which I felt sure must lead back to the river, and had *Heimweh* for England. Not only the England of warm beer and cricket whites and spinsters riding through the mist to Sunday communion. The England of cultures clashing, democratic chaos, of the next musical fad, the ageing punks around World's End, pimpled youths on the tube, the wordless Pakistani grocer fingering out your change. The England of rain, of burnt-out summer piers, of the Chelsea mob baying their way through Soho, the politely lethal policemen hemming them in. I passed a demonstration in a square, of young girls in coloured balaclavas bouncing behind a mass of riot police, a bellowing group of youths outside them, punching the air, it seemed, all in time to a booming music track. And I felt that *Heimweh* again.

So tell me, I said to Istvan, when I entered the office, about the coloured balaclava.

What about it? he asked.

I passed some kind of demonstration.

Kind of pirate copy of Pussy Riot that can be reproduced at will. I blame the internet. Any bunch of pissed-off kids can put on the coloured balaclavas, get boombox and dance around municipal buildings, and what do you know? There is another.

Another what?

Another riot. Police come in with batons and whips, there is overreaction, demonstrations, for and against. The balaclava is a virus, a riot virus.

The gun had not made its reappearance. He was cleaning his sunglasses now.

I can see from your expression, he said to me, that it was a wild-boar chase.

Goose, I corrected him. Wild-goose chase. And yes, there was no Petra. There was a madam, who was quite the anglophile.

Anglophile?

A lover of England, and its peculiar place names. There was a girl called Anya, who seemed in need of an intervention.

She has a drug habit, I elaborated, to his raised eyebrows. If you could persuade the forces of law and order to raid the place, maybe someone could help her.

Is she our concern? he asked me.

She should be somebody's.

There are junkie hookers on every street corner. And at least this one has a room. Is it a small room that she cannot leave?

It didn't seem to be.

So, I keep looking? For another hidden brothel in the twelfth?

If you would.

How English of me, I thought. And I checked my diary and saw I had an appointment.

There were no coloured balaclavas on the boulevard, no whip-wielding Cossacks, just the unrelenting heat and the stalled traffic, and the sound of some fracas way beyond it. So when I made it to his office I was drenched in sweat and Sarah was already on her perch by the half-open window.

You're late, she said.

Sorry, I said, to both of you. I got caught up.

And where were we? the Viennese said, though calling him Viennese is disingenuous, but I'll keep doing so, if I may.

You mentioned the word contempt.

Did I? he asked, and raised his eyebrows and for the first time I observed how outrageously luxuriant they were.

You had detected a certain residual affection between us, which might be enough to save the marriage. And residual affection, you observed, was better than contempt.

I don't remember that word, said Sarah.

Because, darling, you had already left.

You remember everything, observed the therapist.

Yes, I said. It's part of my job. I remember every errant phrase, every crumpled receipt, every gesture of contempt or affection. I remember things, I brood upon them, I pick them apart, I look for signs and symbols in what

I remember. I consider memory the cousin of jealousy and I am, sadly, a jealous man.

And I remember that word, she said. Darling.

Yes, I said. So English, isn't it? It can act like a kiss or a slap in the face. One is never sure which. Do you miss England, Sarah?

Do I miss what, exactly, in England, dear?

The rain? The rationality?

I miss umbrellas, she said, inconsequentially.

Wellington boots.

Bicycles.

It was fun, talking as if the Viennese wasn't there. His enormous eyebrows shifted back and forwards, from me to her.

Harrow-on-the-Hill.

Is it on a hill? asked Sarah.

Apparently.

Always hated Harrow, she said. Pinner. The Metropolitan line.

I understand, he said. The eyebrows nodded. You talk as if I am not here. Good.

You approve? asked Sarah.

My purpose, he said, is to make myself irrelevant.

I understood your purpose to be different, Sarah muttered.

Your understanding of my purpose is?

If I may quote, the conversion of hysterical misery into ordinary unhappiness.

Bravo, Sarah.

Thank you, Jonathan.

I think the phrase was 'neurotic misery', he said.

Neurotic misery then, Sarah said. Let's get back to that.

So soon? I asked.

We are paying, Sarah said and tried to hide her smile.

And I felt he was offended, so brought the conversation back to what seemed was the subject. Misery.

Is there a difference, I asked him, between neurotic and hysterical misery?

Hysteria was a term Freud associates with women, he said.

Hysteria, Sarah said. Womb. Hysterectomy.

Pussy Riot.

My behaviour, therefore, Sarah said, he would have termed hysterical.

The conversation has moved on since then, the doctor said.

I missed him, Sarah said. He was away and I missed him more. I befriended his friend to talk about him. And I end up missing him entirely.

Which is why we are here?

Is that a statement or a question?

Both, I suppose. And his eyebrows were at rest for once.

The thing about England that I miss, said Sarah, is Englishness.

And there is such a thing?

Well, she said, and tapped a coloured nail off one of her teeth, if there were, it would be to do with what's missing in this room.

And what is that?

Understatement, she said. Certain things can be understood, and not necessarily . . .

She raised her head. She examined her beautiful nail.

Talked about.

Can we understand what happens without talking about it?

I can, she said. The question is, can he?

22

When I walked with her down the stairs, she held my arm. She kept holding it, walking down the hot boulevard, and we both seemed to take comfort for a while in saying nothing.

It would be a relief, wouldn't it? she said eventually.

Not to talk?

To be understood.

She kissed me then, at the junction.

I have to pick up Jenny, she said. And you?

I have to work.

You understood me once, she whispered.

I watched her move off among the bobbing pedestrian heads and after a moment I began to follow. That blonde hair above the light summer dress was easy to keep track of and if she turned, though I knew she wouldn't, I had two or three bodies between us behind which to lose myself. Would I understand her again, I wondered, if she led me to something unmentionable, to the thing she was so reluctant to talk about? She turned left then, down that warren of small cobbled streets, and I heard the cello playing and I stopped and let her disappear. She was on her way to pick up Jenny, and I was on my way, following that sound.

Again, the arch with the ceramic tiles, the courtyard, the balconies above. The stone steps, leading up into a mouth of darkness, and the bowed sound echoing round. There was something oriental about that space, a touch of fantasy; it could have lived in Tbilisi or Samarkand. Again, my echoing feet on the stairs the lace curtain drawn and pulled, the Slavic face behind. I walked up slowly, as if I wanted to delay the moment. Again, the door was half-open and it creaked as it let me inside.

And she was sitting on the couch, again, that woman-shaped instrument between her knees. The windows were closed for once and there was a scent in the air.

You wear perfume, I said.

She smiled. Laid aside the bow.

Yes. I am a woman, after all. Why do you mention?

My wife told me I smelt different.

What's your wife's name?

And for some reason I didn't want to tell her, a reason I couldn't fathom. Was it loyalty, guilt, or simple English manners? I asked her to play the thing again.

The fourth suite, she said.

Do you have a favourite? I asked her.

No, she said. But when I get to the sixth . . .

When you get to the sixth, what happens?

Shall we wait and see?

Do you have a husband?

Why you ask?

I asked because he was staring at me. Below on the street, on the opposite pavement, a dark slash against the sunlit wall.

There was a man outside, I said, the last time I left. He's outside again now.

Tell me what he looks like.

He's in a suit. A dark suit. His hair's growing thin. He wears patent-leather shoes.

Grigory, she said, and put the cello to one side. First cellist in the orchestra. He was my teacher.

Was?

Before the love-thing happened.

The love-thing?

The love-thing, she said, is when you say, of all the people in the universe, I am bound to you. I give my memories to you, whatever I know of this world, I give my soul to you, I give you the possibility of hurting me, causing me infinite pain, grief, loss, the total sum of me will be known by you, and if one of us breaks this thing, the other is left unmoored, without reason, friendless, loveless, in a universe of hurt.

Standing in the shadow of the wall below, he seemed a most unlikely repository of all that emotion. I remembered the smell of his towelly robe. And I thought to myself: there is no accounting for taste.

You know the love-thing?

It sounds terrifying, I said.

It is.

And why would anyone want it?

They don't, she said. It happens. You're lying there. Afterwards. You look at the pile of clothes beside the bed. You think, don't those clothes look good together? And you realise that your whole life has been a kind of waiting. For this moment. For this thing.

You're talking about him, I said.

Am I? She turned her head towards me and away again, as if the thought upset her.

And the child you lost was his.

Now that, she said, is true.

Do all women do this? I asked her.

Do what? she asked.

Talk about an absent man with a present one.

Did your wife?

I suspect she did.

She began to stroke the strings again with the bow, softly.

And which were you, she said, above the gathering sound, the absent or the present one?

23

He was present when I descended the steps, waiting in the shadow of the arch. I could have walked across the courtyard to the smaller exit, but I was tired, or I was curious, or just annoyed at being observed. So I continued, through the splash of late-afternoon sunlight, to the tiled wall against which he stood, and there was no cello playing, which I thought was odd. As I passed him he spoke again.

Hey, he said. Or was it how, or you? It was a greeting, whatever he said, designed to arrest one, neither friendly nor unfriendly, just curt. I stopped of course and turned once more and realised I remembered nothing of his face. The clothes I had remembered, the suit, with dampened patches round the armpits now in the summer heat, but I knew nothing of the face and wondered had it been because my eyes avoided it.

But there it was now, in the shadow, against the ceramic wall, dark, almost Levantine, slightly pockmarked round the cheeks and with a broad, full mouth. And I felt a pang of jealousy until I realised how absurd the feeling was.

You. It was you, he said, not hey this time. So the hey must have come first.

This was the love-object, yet another one. And I found myself wondering did he favour cufflinks.

Yes, I said.

No music today.

Not now. It seems to have stopped.

How can it just stop?

It comes and goes, I said, and tried to move on my way.

Please, he said. Tell me. What you do up there.

And there was panic in his voice, or something like desperation. I realised, with a dull sense of surprise, that he might be jealous too.

Nothing, I said.

Nothing?

I talk, I suppose.

Just talk?

And when I don't talk, I listen.

Talk about what?

It would be impolite, I told him, to share that with you.

I don't know, he said. Impolite.

It's an English term, I told him.

Perhaps you are being ... foolish.

I am sure of it, I said. And I must go now. If you'll excuse me.

And he did. He stepped aside, and let me pass. I walked through the arch, on to the blissfully shaded street, and found a corner shop and ducked inside. I bought some gum from the proprietress, and saw his dark hair move past the window, then I walked back out. And I did what I was trained to do: I followed him, and kept half a length of street between us.

He made it through the cobbled streets to the wider boulevard and walked in the shade of the trees that flanked the traffic lane. I stayed on the pavement. I kept one eye on his dark suit as it appeared and disappeared behind the gleaming windows of the fitfully moving traffic.

Following. I could write a book on it. I probably am. It is one of the basic pleasures of the trade, like the feel of wood to a carpenter or of engine oil to a mechanic; it has its rhythms, its own moods, its basic quotidian duties and its sudden surprises. There's a kind of Zen peace to it, it works best in a city, of course, along crowded boulevards like this one, where the parallax of passing bodies, lampposts, trees and traffic provide not only a cover but a kind of intermittent beat, an interrupted rhythm to the follower's eye. There are the city sounds, of course, the blaring horns, the click clack of passing heels, the murmured conversations between businessmen, friends and lovers with who knows what endearments, emotional, financial, collegial. World after world passes the follower by and he – or she – has one ear out for those snatches of contingent lives, with one eye always on the subject – generally beyond hearing. You fall into an observant lull, the kind of peace a child has when it plays in a lonely sandpit; you forget yourself, your name, your anxieties and cares, you immerse yourself entirely in that other, that thing that is not you, that walks these city streets with a purpose, a destiny, a home, a family, a lover, all of which it may be your duty to discover.

So he was walking, through the aisle of linden trees, until he came to what seemed like a shell made of concrete rising out of the pavement, and he took a series of steps downward and vanished from sight. I sidestepped through the traffic and saw a metro entrance, the dark shape vanishing sideways, the hot-enginey wind blowing upwards into my face. Of course I followed, and found him on a platform with a random group of tourists in the grinding subway heat, as if all of the day's humidity had gathered itself down here into one hot, fetid cloud. A train came, which he let pass, and then another, which he took. I jumped on the carriage behind, and could see the back of his head through the rear window, appearing and disappearing in the contrary motion of the carriages.

Why was I following? I had no idea. For the pure pleasure of it, I suppose. I was a follower. One of those who latches on to a life that seems more urgent than their own. It was habit, and I was curious. To know the story that had driven her to that bridge, to get some inkling into what she called the love-thing. To see did he wear cufflinks too.

And the train swayed and slowed and I saw him grab the handrail and saw the frayed cuff of his shirt and knew that he didn't. Not that it mattered anyway. But the shirt was poor and maybe he was too. What did a cellist earn in an opera orchestra in this backward place? I had no idea.

The train shuddered, coming to some destination, and I felt a sudden, irrational surge of panic that the station would be my own. I had never taken the train home; the car was a necessity, what with schools and music lessons. What if I followed him up a set of steps, down a winding

street and saw him enter a faux-wooden Tyrolean structure
that was my own? What if Sarah was home and embraced
him with a familiar hug, a kiss, brought him through that
heavy door for an hour or two of questionable pleasure? It
was absurd, I knew, but out of the lulled daydreams of the
follower's mind, all sorts of strange fancies emerge. Most of
them are useless, but the follower entertains them because
one in a thousand might turn out to be true. And the train
came to a halt at an unfamiliar station, and I saw him elbow
his way to the carrriage door and walk with a distracted air
down a suburban platform towards another set of steps.
And of course I followed.

We emerged into the hot, dying day. On a steeply rising
cobbled street, almost medieval, with façades on either side
that seemed to lean towards each other, as if their gutters
and gables wanted to touch. And maybe one day they
would. There was three hundred years of leaning in these
structures, the tiny windows crushed out of shape by the
weight of brick above them, and the roofs had lost all
semblance of anything like a straight line. The sun was
setting and there was an amber glow to the light that
remained. A tiny sliver of its reddened ball was all that was
left of it behind the dark silhouetted mass of a castle rising
above those layers of irregular rooftop. And he walked
down this street without a thought, as if it was his own.

His shoes echoed on the cobbled surface. An older
woman with a headscarf passed him and nodded in some
kind of recognition. So people lived on these medieval
streets, they were more than picture-perfect postcards; they
were home, at least to him.

He turned left now, down a narrower street, though one wouldn't have thought it possible. But there it was, a dark ribbon of cobbles among single-storey houses, and he took a key from his pocket and opened a door and walked inside one of them.

I stood on the corner for a breath or two. I heard the woman walk back the way we had come. I watched the sun vanish completely behind the dark shape of the castle. And I heard another sound then, a rhythmic creaking, and realised it came from the door above the house. It was a small wooden sign, and it was angling backwards and forwards. There was no breeze, so it must have been the motion of the door as he entered that caused it to move. I walked towards it, slowly, after what seemed like a decent enough interval. There was faded handwritten lettering on the wooden sign. It spelled, in faux-medieval Germanic letters: *Musikinstrumente*.

Why the German, I had no idea. But it was a sign, and it advertised a shop, a tiny one, which I had to observe through the small, almost crushed windows. I could see musical shapes, inside, of a cello, a viola, a violin. I could see shelves stacked with sheet music for sale. And I could see him making his way past a counter, through this elongated room into another room inside. And in there I could see a woman and a child seated at a kitchen table.

He had a wife, of course. He ran a music shop to supplement his income from the orchestra. And he had a child, and hadn't wanted another.

24

She was late home and of course I wondered why. But a simple sentence like that conveys nothing of the turmoil the fact gave rise to. I cooked a meal for Jenny and tried to occupy my mind by laying out a separate plate for each of her imaginary friends. There were three of them, as far as I could remember. Melanie, Jessica and a third whose name always escaped me. I cooked a simple pasta and the chopping of the onions made me cry. She was practising inside on her violin, the halting finger scales that bore very little relationship to music, when they changed into a gentle arpeggio that she repeated and repeated, as if practising for a school concert.

What's that? I asked her.

It's the cello thing, she said. That the lady played.

Ah, I thought and then felt guilty that I had taken her down that street, let her hear that sound.

I've laid out plates, I told her, for Melanie and Jessica but I can't remember the third name.

Rebecca, she said.

Will they all take Parmesan cheese? I asked.

No, she said. Melanie's lactose intolerant. Jessica and Rebecca are on a diet.

Ah. The same diet? I asked.

No dairy, she said, continuing with the same arpeggio. Do da dee da dee da dee da do da dee da dee da dee da.

And you? I asked. You are the important one, after all.

Parmesan for me, she said and laid down her violin and bow and walked through the inner door.

Where's Mummy? she asked.

Working, I imagine. So it's just the two of us.

Daddy! Tut tut.

Sorry. The five of us.

Was it a game that she played that had become too real? Or was it a childhood reality that she would soon grow out of? If it was a game, it was fun to play it, the pretence of laying a precise ladle of pasta on every plate, with a spoonful of sauce and a small conversation about each invisible one's eating habits.

Jessica thinks you should make it up with her.

But we've never fallen out.

Yes you have. Jessica says you can't hide things from her.

Why would I fall out with Jessica?

Not with Jessica. With Mummy.

Ah.

That loaded word again. I thought about it while we both ate.

But I have made it up with her.

No you haven't. You say you have but you haven't.

Darling, you know Mummy and Daddy love each other.

She thought for a moment, then twisted some bands of spaghetti on her fork until they were uniformly red.

Jessica says that sometimes that's not enough.

Oh dear. Jessica had far too much insight into domestic affairs.

Has she been watching those TV programmes?

You mean the ones where the couples shout at each other over the man with the white hair?

The Jerry Springer Show? Yes, I suppose I do.

I resolved to supervise her television diet more thoroughly. But I began to realise how useful Jessica was as a conduit into my daughter's thoughts.

She watches it sometimes.

And she knows that she's not meant to? It's for adults.

Then why is it on in the daytime?

Why? I had no idea.

Tell her your mother and your father are nothing like those couples. We don't pull each other's hair and fight on television.

But, she said.

But what? I asked her.

Nothing, she said and filled her mouth with spaghetti. Maybe so she wouldn't have to continue the subject.

I want to learn it, she said, eventually.

What? I asked.

That tune, the woman plays.

Bach, I told her. The cello suites.

And I pressed a button on the CD player, and the sober sound of Casals filled the room.

It sounds different, she said.

Yes. This is a man who died a long time ago.

Ah, she said. Maybe that explains it. I don't like this. I prefer the woman.

What woman? I asked. And maybe I was fishing, to find out what she knew, or what she could intuit.

The woman we heard playing, on the way to music. Jessica says she sounds like jealous.

The cellist, I said.

And Jessica hears her too?

She looked at me and smiled, with a mouth reddened with sauce, and said nothing more.

I had her in bed by the time Sarah came back.

Forgive me, she said, with the kind of formality that implied there was something to forgive. I got caught in a riot.

Nothing dangerous, I hope.

Nothing like Mesopotamia, she said.

She liked the classical term. It blunted the reality of charred bodies and severed heads.

The dig, she said. We had to shift a tree. A crowd gathered. The tree is sacred, apparently. A vapis.

A what?

We left under police escort. Riot shields, tear gas, the works.

You want some food?

Please.

She sat. I filled a plate. There was a smudge of mud on her forehead.

You got hurt?

She shook her head.

A rumour spread. About the body in the bog.

The girl.

That it's a boy. St Panteleimon. That the wounds are marks of persecution.

St who?

A martyr, under Diocletian. Sacred to one side or the other.

And is it?

No. It's a girl. From centuries before. Early Bronze Age. But. They want excuses. To throw things at each other.

No killing.

Not yet.

25

I lay awake and watched her sleep. Not so much watched, really, as felt. I listened to the rise and fall of her breathing, inhaled that musty odour of hairspray, face cream and day-old beauty products, together with something older and more primal, a mixture of clay and newly mown grass. If I turned my head to the side I could see her profile, against the dim, cream-coloured wall behind. She slept on her back that night. She normally slept sideways, her body curled into a curve that used to match mine. Her finger brushed off her nose in her sleep, as if an invisible fly had irritated it. She shifted her head and said the word 'church' as if she was dreaming of one. I took her hand in her sleep and brought it close to my face. I could see the dark line of something underneath her painted nails and wondered if it was clay from the dig.

I had the kind of dreams that felt like waking. There was a naked body with skin the texture of leather trying to rise from a riverbed of slime. It was as thin as a handbag or the kinds of chaps that rodeo riders wear. The hands curled round my face like old calfskin gloves and the legs wrapped round mine like broad flaps of seaweed underwater.

I awoke to find her already dressed, bringing Jenny's face to mine in a goodbye kiss.

We're late, she said. And it seemed you needed to sleep. I'll do the necessaries.

And then they were gone.

There was a strange peace in the house with its Tyrolean pretensions and its garden through the French windows with the parched grass and the linden or laurel trees. A car drifted by outside with its horn pressed in a long wail that reminded me of the cry of a peacock. We had walked through a ransacked palace in the months when we first met and the same damaged cry echoed round the empty halls and there was a miniature zoo visible through the windows with the ruined walls and cages and a peacock took to the air and flapped its way to freedom, its tail hanging backwards like a feathered diadem. I rolled out of bed and was washing my teeth when my mobile rang and I saw the name Frank come up on the display. I went to turn it off and must have pressed the wrong icons because a GPS map of the city revealed itself, with a pulsating red dot, and I remembered the system we had installed, with their mutual tracking devices, so that each phone could situate the other. So I knew where he was now, I realised with a kind of dull, subdued surprise, and I wondered why I hadn't used such a tool when I most needed it. I poured myself juice and cereal and was drinking tea and chewing the crust of a piece of buttered toast when I saw the dot begin to shift and realised he was on the move.

I drove into the city then, and kept one eye on that red dot and its movements. I kept the phone perched by the dashboard and saw it was moving as slowly as I was, approaching the river from the other side, stuck in a matching lane of traffic. In the future, I thought, we will all be traceable at all times and then I realised, with whatever is the opposite of déjà vu, that this future had already arrived. Was I following him? No, not yet. I was merely following a similar path to his. Jealousy, like love, works in strange ways. It's only after some time that we come to realise we are living under its influence. So I drove as I would have driven any normal day until I saw that his red dot had stalled, somewhere on the river's left bank, and I put two and two together and realised he was parking his car. So I parked mine. I walked then, along the grey concrete banks, and kept pace with his dot as I moved along the opposite side. He was heading towards the suspension bridge with the huge metal hawsers arcing from the giant pillars and the stone angels blindly facing the river below. I walked up the stone steps under the archway and lost the signal for a moment, under the weight, I supposed, of the granite from above. So I kept walking up and the red dot reappeared, coming towards me now, so I walked across the traffic to the opposite side. I walked through the morning crowds, the buskers already squatting on their chosen spots, the young businessmen with the short white sleeves and the designer backpacks, the cyclists dodging the mid-morning tourists, and then I saw him for real, silhouetted against the green water, walking the other way. There was a purpose to his stride, but no particular speed. Then his mobile must have buzzed, because he took it from his pocket and began to talk to someone as he walked. I stopped and watched him pass me by. If he had turned he would have waved, I suppose, in some collegiate greeting, crossed the road to speak to me, and asked how things were going. But thankfully he didn't. The conversation kept him engrossed, kept his head to one side, and I crossed the road and followed.

So I was a follower again, a real one; he was five or six pedestrians in front of me and as he approached the steps I had ascended, he looked to his left and waved to somebody on the riverbank below.

I looked down and immediately wished I hadn't. But I had known what the outcome would be, I suppose, when I began following that red dot. It would be something to do with her. It would be everything to do with her. If it had been someone else down there, waiting for him, it would have still been to do with her. But it wasn't someone else, it was Sarah. She was wearing the clothes she had left the house in, with a new addition, a straw sunhat which shaded her face and the phone that she held to her ear. She looked up. She nodded, but she didn't wave. And I stepped back behind the shield of oncoming pedestrians in case she saw me too.

He walked on, and walked down, and soon vanished. She stood there, waiting, and looked down at her feet and kicked a pebble into the water. There was a barely perceptible splash. She was quite alone down there, on that band of cement littered with detritus from the river. She waited, her shoulders slumped, something sad about her posture, and I felt sorry for her, from my perch way above, as if she was as lost and as lonely as I was. As he was, perhaps. I remembered how I had pulled the girl to the other cement walkway on the other side. Then he appeared beneath the bridge, a lean dark shadow walking towards her, and I turned away. However they would greet each other, I didn't want to see it.

It was only love, after all, no one had died, the crime was the familiar one and the only victims were ourselves. I felt a strange, wintry sense of release and didn't like it at all. I was cold, for some odd reason, in that city heat. I wanted to lie down. I wanted to sleep. I wanted anything but the skin I had to live in.

And so I walked. I was following nothing now, just a remembered sound. I crossed to the other side and traced my way through the boulevards to the tiny streets where I had heard it first. But there was nothing playing. I found the courtyard, walked up the stone steps to the now silent door. I pushed it. It was open. And when I entered, there was no one inside.

There was the sofa, without the cello. There was the open door to the bathroom. There was the bedroom inside, with the mattress on the floor. And I lay down on that mattress and did what I should have done last night. I slept.

26

I dreamt of an entanglement of limbs in brown soupish water. Hair like green weeds drifting over my face. A woman naked under a pink ski mask, the open black O of her mouth, into which I was sinking. She was bound to a shower rail by a golden cord and the water whipped down on her from the silver spigot.

It was mid-afternoon when I awoke. Or so the band of sunlight pouring through the window told me. There were tiny fragments of dust wheeling in the sunlight, and a buzzing mosquito. I reached out to grab it, but it arced away from my hand as if it already knew my intention.

I heard the sound of falling water, like the last breath of the dream I had come out of, but it didn't go away, it persisted. I turned my head to the bathroom door and saw the glass of the shower fogged up with steam, the shape of a woman behind it. The shape moved and a hand grabbed a towel and the towel was pink and she emerged, her head bound in this pink towel like an unruly turban. She was naked underneath it and everything was suddenly real, too real. She knelt down on the sheet that covered me and unwrapped the weight of her body around me, underneath it.

You felt free enough to let yourself in.

I did. I'm sorry.

Why sorry? It was good to find you here. Asleep, mid-day. Like you were home.

Home?

And it was even better to lie down beside you. And, you know.

So, I had not been dreaming. But it would have been impolite to mention that. So I said what anyone would say.

Yes.

She pulled the towel off and turned her head.

Help me dry.

And I rubbed her hair between two bands of pink towel.

They look good together, she said.

And I remembered she had said that before. But I repeated, almost ritually: What?

Our clothes.

They were lying on the bare wooden boards. Mine, and above them hers. A thin yellow summer dress, like the Pussy Rioters wore.

I was taking the last few steps from the stairs to the fanciful courtyard when the cello started up again from above. A summery baroque dance, which I later came to recognise as the gigue from suite four. It was precise and light, exact as a piece of lacework, and I was imagining her fingers stopping on the strings when my mobile rang and the office number showed up. I heard Istvan on the line.

Where have you been? he asked. I have news.

Sleeping, I told him.

Well, come round, he said. You have an office, remember? And what used to be a business.

So I continued on through the arch where the summery gigue was drowned out by the sound of a distant riot.

It was another demonstration on the boulevard. The coloured balaclavas bounced up and down behind masses of police helmets, which separated them from a baying crowd in camouflage and combat clothing. It was like an unruly gymnastic display, and I was amazed at their level of fitness. Thin, muscular arms, dressed in pink and yellow tank tops, under the bobbing, pastel-coloured ski masks. Maybe they sold them in Benetton.

I found Istvan at his desk, with his back turned towards me. He swivelled his chair around when I entered.

It is strange, he said, how battle lines take shape. We always thought it would be Russophiles and nationalists, the old pre-war divisions making space for themselves again. The Jew on one side, the Christian on the other, Catholic, Orthodox, atheist, Muslim, anarchist all falling into line, on one side or the other. But who could have foreseen the coloured balaclava? It spreads like its own virus, creating new fault lines altogether, new orthodoxies, throwing church into the arms of a state it used to hate, internationalist and nationalist band together against this degendered neutered thing that believes in nothing but street sex and boomboxes in public places and wants to turn this place we know into some Strasbourgian Nordic version of permanent disco night.

You won't be wearing the coloured one, I gather.

And now, he went on, with a kind of worldly Slavic sadness, there are rumours, that they have found the grave of St Panteleimon.

And that's significant?

Martyr. Roman times. Patron saint of the church of Constantine. A discovery that could have united us all.

And will it?

He blew through his closed lips.

There are no more brothels to be found in the twelfth, by the way. Of all the districts in the city, it is quite unusually chaste.

And that was your news?

No. My news was this.

He turned his laptop towards me.

There was a small, unremarkable building on the screen, with lettering above the door.

What does it read? I asked.

Morga, he said. City morgue.

Of course, it would come down to that. One knows without admitting it; one looks from the Polaroid of little Petra to the enduring faces of her parents and thinks what one cannot say. Save your money, she's already dead.

You think she's inside there? I asked him. And there was a dead feeling inside me.

What did the psychic tell you?

That she was in a small room that she cannot leave.

Well. It has many small rooms. That the residents cannot leave.

He was really going for the Yorick thing today. But it suited him somehow, those Slavic jowls and the moonlike glasses. Maybe he had found his voice.

Can we go there?

Not without appointment. It is a morgue, after all. And Jonathan?

He pronounced it the Gertrude way. Three syllables. Jo-na-than.

Yes?

Frank called.

I sat at my desk with my back to him. Of course he would call. One day.

He thinks you two should talk.

Perhaps we should, I thought. A have-a-drink kind of talk.

He's in a bar around the corner.

I opened my desk drawer and saw the Glock sitting there. Like all guns, it seemed to want to be put to use. Some day.

And what would Frank be? A coloured balaclava or a black?

Balaclava is not Frank's style.

I slipped it into my waistband and stood, and found a jacket on the wall. I put that on, even though it was too hot.

Which bar?

He mentioned a name. An unfamiliar one.

I walked out and the gun walked with me. I remembered the feeling very well.

27

So there he was, dressed in a linen waistcoat and an immaculate pale-green shirt with short sleeves. So the cufflinks weren't an issue, thank God. He was sitting by a scarred wooden bar in a room with bare brick walls and no glass in the windows. It was a style they had there: take a ruin and design a bar around it. He smiled when he saw me enter, and then looked behind me and smiled again, apologetically, as if to say here was his appointment, and any new acquaintance would have to wait. I assumed there was a woman behind me, or several; he was that kind of man, after all, to whom women came easily. But I wasn't so indelicate as to turn; I would save that for later. I kept my jacket on and sat down beside him and asked him if it came to balaclavas, which colour would he wear.

Strange greeting, he said.

Strange times, I said.

Yes, I agree, he said. We'll all be at it soon.

Killing? I asked.

Barricading. Burning tyres. First things first.

I was in Dubrovnik, I said, before the thing broke there. They would point across the bar at friends who would soon be cut-throat enemies. They would smile, shake hands.

I was making small talk and I wasn't sure why. And he was good enough to stop me.

You've got to stop blaming her, he said. Blame me.

For what? I asked.

Aha, he said. That's the thing, isn't it?

Why are we even having this conversation?

He looked over my shoulder again. And this time I had to turn.

Do you think I want it? he asked softly.

There was a girl by a stool, at the bare brick wall. She looked like a student. She caught my eye and looked away.

Because, he was saying, she asked me to.

She asked you when?

Yesterday, he said. I met her by the river.

And so, I thought. I was wrong about that, too. How many more things could I be wrong about?

And if you want to hit me, he said, now is probably a good time.

And I could have, I suppose. I could have whacked him once and watched his head bounce off the scarred wooden bartop. By the time he brought it up again I could have had the Glock out and decorated the whole place with him. But it seemed strangely inappropriate. He looked sad and tired of the whole business.

She wanted to talk, he said. She missed you. She still misses you. She even wanted me to teach her how to say it my way.

How? I asked him.

Chybis mi, he said. And if it sounds flirtatious, it is only because I am that kind of man. The kind of man women want to flirt with, when they want it to mean nothing. I am the great nothing, the great vacuum. I listen and I nod and I smile in appreciation and every now and then it works for me, I get into their favour, but your wife, my good friend, was not one of those.

I was not his friend, not any longer, but I took his cue and listened and I nodded and was amazed at what self-laceration it gave rise to.

You were hardly there. You gave me a lesson, actually, in loving, if it ever should come to that with someone and me, because you had assumed an intimacy you no longer bothered to practise, you left her with me to choose office furniture, an indication if there ever was one of lost interest, lack of interest, you no longer bothered even to be jealous, and jealousy, she told me, was inseparable from her idea of love.

She told you this where?

In the bar of that concrete place by the water. We had drinks and a laughable attempt at dinner. I booked a room which she paid for to keep the conversation going and the suggestion was mine, not hers. I wanted to know what it meant to be loved, to be cherished, to be the cause of such bereavement. I wanted to be you for a while and I failed miserably. But I did what you mustn't have done for so long. I listened.

A present one and an absent one, I thought. And I kept my mouth shut.

I would have worn your clothes if they had been avail-able, just to know what it felt like. Because I am a man, not like you. I am the one they want to fuck, when they want it to mean nothing. I am the one they can leave without a thought or a backward glance, thinking that was nice. The one with the smooth body and the shaved chest, and I know you've noticed that, because I heard you say so. So I wanted to be in the clothes of a marriage, if only to know what it felt like. And I have to say, it felt good, while it lasted.

You should stop there, I told him.

And thank you for saying that. I should stop there. You want to know how long it lasted?

No, I said. I think you've said enough.

Too much, he said. I'm a listener, not a talker. So tell me, he continued, tell me what went wrong; maybe your eye had wandered, maybe there was another one too, one like me that you leave in the morning and want to oblit-erate from memory.

An absent one, I thought.

It was good, he said, being you for a while, for a few hours, but I was never the husband, I didn't even come close, I was hardly the lover. You are both of those things for her and I am the jealous one, oddly enough. You should leave that bile and that envy to me. You must keep being the husband, my friend, and do what the husband does.

What does the husband do?

He – what is the phrase? He makes up. He knows the dislocation was his, maybe the fault was his and the love is all his, if he wants it. He buys her something. Something with sentimental associations. A gift.

He lit a cigarette. He offered me one. I shook my head.

Tell me just one thing, I said. Why did she pay the bill?

And he smiled. If he was to be undone, it would be by vanity.

Because with me, he said, the woman always pays. And she has paid, I assume.

She told you?

No. Her face said it all.

He smiled. He brushed his eyes, as if the cigarette smoke was bringing water to them. I assumed it was that, and not tears. It was odd, to feel so close to someone so repellent. But I had worked with him once and tolerated him and maybe would do so again. What was odder was to have Sarah in common with him. As if she was a pool and we were both doing laps, up and down.

I said goodbye and passed the girl who looked like a student, in her high stool against the bare brick wall, and saw her look up at someone, not me.

28

The boulevard was empty of traffic when I walked back down it. There was the smell of tear gas in the summer air and random groups of policemen stood under the linden trees, sweating under their visors in the intolerable heat. There was no more sign of riot, though, and whatever passers-by there were kept to the shaded side of the street. I saw a yellow balaclava hanging on a parking meter, streaked with the colour pink. I picked it up, saw the round open O of the mouth and realised the pink was the stain of blood, some young girl's blood. Or boy's, since it was impossible to tell, under those pastel-coloured ski masks, which may have been the point. The blood and the bright childish yellow made a miserable contrast and I dropped it, as if it had been some young thing's undergarment, which again may have been the point. Blood and pastel.

Some of the shop windows were broken, their owners patiently sweeping up the shattered glass, as if they had done it before and would soon be doing it again. I passed a jeweller's, with miraculously unbroken plate-glass windows behind a metal mesh, and saw a display behind it, gleaming pinpoints of white light against a green baize cloth. There was a bracelet there, of black pearls curled into a figure of eight. And I thought maybe he was right, it was time, the man should do what the man does and buy his wife something with sentimental associations. A gift.

I walked inside and thought of opera and pearls, and wondered why. That opera by Bizet, *The Pearl Fishers*, with its duet that I had always found so anodyne. Did Sarah ever like it? I couldn't remember. But I knew she liked pearls, black ones particularly, and I was reaching through to the window display to take them out, when the shop assistant came up behind me.

Let me, she said.

I stood obediently back and she hooked them round her finger, and held them up to the sunlight coming through the window.

You like pearls?

My wife does, I said.

Black pearls. Japanese. Uncultured.

I can see that, I said.

You know pearls?

I shook my head.

You know the duet, though. *The Pearl Fishers*.

Was this a sales pitch, I wondered, or some kind of osmosis. Then she nodded her head, to the building across the street, and I understood.

I heard Andrea Bocelli sing it over there. In the State Opera. He was blind, so had no idea how beautiful the setting was.

I could see it through the grilled mesh. A fin-de-siècle attempt at grandeur, like a miniature of the Garnier in Paris.

His voice, though, was even better.

Better than what? I asked.

Than the beautiful setting. That he couldn't see. You've been inside? The opera?

Never, I said.

Though I must have passed it so many times without even a glance.

Well, you should visit. Though maybe it closed, with the trouble on the street.

You like pearls? she asked again. Black pearls? You want to read about them?

She turned and took a small booklet from the counter.

A symbol of hope, it says here. For wounded hearts.

Aha.

And every heart is wounded. Once or twice.

Is that you talking now, or the booklet?

Me, she said. And she held the pearls up against her salmon-coloured blouse.

Your wife's colouring? Like mine?

A little, I said, although I didn't mean it. She had the palest of skin, like a nun's.

May I?

I took the booklet from her hand and saw how expensive they were.

We can talk of discount, she said, again reading my thoughts. If you pay cash.

I've only credit cards.

Even so, she said.

29

I walked out with a small carefully wrapped box dangling from my index finger. The smell of tear gas was gone from the air and the traffic had once more begun its slow crawl. I crossed the street, weaving between out-of-date cars until I reached the opera steps. The heavy wooden doors were open and there was a man in uniform between them with a leather wallet round his neck. And as I mounted the steps I wondered why I'd never noticed it before. Because I had the philistine's dislike of opera: warbling sopranos and pearl-fishing duets. Maybe, but the building had a lot to recommend it and I liked old buildings: looking at them, wandering through them, thinking about them. Two caryatids stood on either side of him, supporting the carved arch above the door.

No opera tour today, he said, though I hadn't asked for one. And when I asked him why, he said, The demonstration. But if I paid the recommended contribution, I could walk around with an audio guide. So I walked inside, into the carved-stone interior, and paid the woman behind the glass cabinet the recommended fee.

There was another grand staircase before me with a carpet of a red so bright it almost hurt the eyes. It branched off, to the left and right, and the balustrades rose and drew the eye to a bewildering series of murals above. Overhanging trees, ivy, collapsing ruins and follies, nymphs, fauns and cupids with faded pink bodies, that all seemed frozen in the act of tumbling down towards me. There was a large decorative arch beneath them that led to what I knew must be the auditorium, so I climbed up to it and underneath and found myself among long rows of empty seats with gilded boxes rising above them in a semicircle, at the end of which was the empty stage with the huge red curtains drawn back. The only light in there was the sunlight, coming through the circular windows way, way above. So the seats seemed to vanish into a bowl of shadow that led to the stage and the dull gleam of theatrical flats.

I heard a bow scrape over an open string and knew the sound intimately, immediately. It continued on, into an operatic flurry. Someone was playing the cello in the orchestra pit.

I walked forwards, almost blindly, feeling my way by the satin-covered seats that led down the aisle. The cello played again, another operatic flurry, which confused me. I had become so used to Bach. Then the darkness must have softened somewhat, from the sunlight above, or else my eyes had grown used to it. I could see the red-satin covers to the seats, a balustrade at the end of them with a long cushion of red, and as I moved forwards I could see a serried row of music stands, each with a red backing. Was red the only colour that opera allowed? I wondered, and the cello continued and then I saw her, sitting on a gold-painted chair, alone in the orchestra pit, her head raised towards a score on a music stand, the dark hair masking half of her face.

I have to learn this, she said. It's the cello solo from *Rigoletto*.

She must have seen me coming down the aisle, because she spoke without turning.

Act One. Played with the basses.

So your sabbatical is over?

I hope so. Soon. And you? What brought you here?

She looked round then, as she played. What light there was caught her face as the hair fell away from it.

The opera? Made you think of me?

Yes, I said. And I wondered whether it really had or not.

Come down here, she said. Turn the pages.

There was a small recess, an opening in the balustrade. I pushed it back and walked down the narrow steps. I was in the pit then, with the empty music stands and a view of the gilded boxes way up above.

I can't read music.

When I nod, you turn.

And she nodded, so I turned the page of indecipherable squiggles and dots.

Do you know *Rigoletto*?

I shook my head.

It's about a curse.

About how we're all cursed, one way or another?

How did you know?

I didn't. I just said it. Isn't that what all operas are about?

No. Rhinemaidens come up from the water. Orfeo descends into the underworld. Mimi dies from consumption.

And Rigoletto?

He tries to protect his daughter from the Duke. But the curse outwits him. And you turn now.

So I turned the page again. And the wrapped parcel brushed off her cheek.

You bought me something?

I didn't know what to say.

You bought your wife something?

And again, I said nothing. She played two double-stopped notes.

And then the baritone takes over.

Baritone what?

The voice. Rigoletto. The dwarf.

She put aside her bow.

Can I see?

And she had the golden string off my finger in one deft move. She peeled aside the folded paper.

What are they? she asked.

Pearls, I said.

You bought pearls for me?

Black pearls, I said.

Are they bad luck? Are they cursed, like Rigoletto?

She had the pearls out now, and was twisting them around her wrist.

They have bumps on them. Not smooth.

No, I said. They're Japanese. Uncultured.

Why black pearls?

Because, I said, helplessly, and I quoted the brochure, they're a symbol of hope.

Hope?

For wounded hearts.

And tears suddenly sprang from her eyes, like a procession of wet jewels. I had never seen a reaction so immediate. We were in an opera house, I tried to reason, surrounded by the colour crimson. Operatic emotions only.

Thank you, she said.

And I wondered had I enough credit to buy another set.

Kiss me, she said. The way the Duke kissed Gilda.

How did the Duke kiss Gilda?

As if he would die for her.

You mean operatically?

Not funny, she said.

She brought her hand to my face and I kissed her. I felt the pearls against my earlobe.

There now, she said. We're cursed.

By whom?

Not whom. What. We're cursed by the love-thing.

Can we lift the curse?

Never, she said. And there was the sound of voices, doors opening way behind us.

You must go now. Orchestral rehearsal.

I can't sit and listen?

No, she said.

So I climbed the wooden stairs and left her there. I walked back through the shadowed auditorium, past a gathering in the foyer of men and women with instrumental cases. There were more of them on the opera-house steps, smoking in the afternoon heat. I saw the one I had followed, carrying a battered cello case, and he stopped, as if to continue an interrupted conversation. But I excused myself and hurried on.

As I crossed the street, he stood by the wooden doors, staring at me. The rest of the orchestra pushed by him with their oddly shaped cases, as if they contained outsize varieties of vegetables: mushrooms, carrots and courgettes. He stood there, staring, with his battered case which looked like it enclosed a Jerusalem artichoke, until I had lost myself in the foliage of the trees on the other side.

30

I bought a fish on the way home. I had Jenny in the car – it was my turn to pick her up – and stopped outside a fishmonger's. As we walked past the dead-eyed things on the slabs of marble, I realised I was used to sea creatures. Bream, bass, mullet and plaice. Here we had carp and gar and pike and trout, all from rivers and green, muddy lakes. I chose a thing called a zander, or a pike-perch, and saw it lifted from the ice and wrapped in clear plastic and wondered was I doing this because someone else had taken the thing I should have given her.

Why are we cooking fish? Jenny asked.

Because Mummy likes a surprise, I told her.

No she doesn't.

And I realised she was right. That the thing about people who know each other is that they know each other. Whatever love may exist between them has already been mediated by what they know of each other. The unexpected action, the wanted or unwanted gesture, happens on a landscape of anticipated sameness, so the simple and safe course of their day must now be interrupted by some obstacle they have to climb. And while the unexpected is so often what is demanded – by self-help books, magazine articles and marriage therapists – it causes problems of its own. And I wondered, was I going quietly mad? The pearls were a worry. But the fish was an absurdity.

I cooked her a bouillabaisse once.

What's that?

A Provençal fish stew.

And that's what this is for?

She stared at the dead eye through the clear plastic. It was obscuring itself in vapour, as if the fish was breathing.

I thought I'd bake it in garlic and lemon, with a few olives maybe, lots of onions.

What's it called?

A pike-perch. They swear it's a delicacy here.

Butter, the fishmonger said bluntly.

Butter?

Is best with butter. Just butter. Fried in butter.

Maybe butter, then, I said.

Fish with butter, Jenny whispered on the way out. Sounds horrible.

So it does, I agreed. I'll pull up a recipe for baking it on the internet. You can feed me the instructions.

Feed you, she said.

While I skin and chop and peel. It's called cooking. She'll love us for it.

She loves us anyway, she said, with the odd wisdom children have.

And I was thinking of that odd wisdom when I turned left and found myself in a line of stalled cars with some kind of fracas in between them. There must have been a demonstration up ahead, a riot or an event, because they came running through the cars like multicoloured hornets, some of their balaclavas already red with paint or blood, followed by the khaki-coloured storm troopers. One of them leapt on the bonnet of the car in her hiking boots and gave a strange throaty cry. It could have been a whoop of triumph or a scream of pain. Her coloured dress was ripped and I caught a glimpse of a muscular torso and realised that the she might well have been a he. Whatever the gender, she was athletic, because she crossed bonnet after bonnet like a competitive hurdler and had vanished down a side-street before the khaki ones could touch her. And the police behind them, with their velcroed flak jackets and their Perspex shields, were hopelessly late. Then the traffic began to move again, slowly, and I heard the dull thump of drum and bass and saw a Special Forces member in a black balaclava climbing a statue's pedestal, trying to reach the speaker that had been perched above its muscular arm. The hand of the arm held a gigantic hammer, a symbol of some industry long dead now, and the electric cord of the speaker was wrapped round the bronze wrist. So they had performed their absurd dance and drawn a crowd and an outraged counter-demonstration and a flotilla of police vans to subdue the subsequent riot and on it went. I was thinking of Istvan's comments on the genius of the coloured balaclava when Jenny spoke from behind and asked me where she could buy those facemasks.

Why do you want one? I asked.

Not one, she said. Three or four. So we can all do the dance.

And as I parked the car, she pogoed up the driveway towards the Tyrolean house. I imagined three disembodied coloured balaclavas pogoing with her.

So we cooked. I deboned the fish and chopped the onions and garlic and wrapped the lot in greased paper and placed it in the baking oven. Jenny washed a salad and Sarah came in late and we ate the resultant dish to the sound of Pablo Casals.

Why do you always play that? Jenny asked.

Because I found it by accident and I want to listen to them through, from beginning to end. And it's good for you to listen to great music.

That was Sarah, not me. But I could have asked the same question.

How's the fish? I asked. I found the flesh buttery and slightly wet and I was glad I hadn't heeded the fishmonger.

It's brilliant, she said. An unexpected treat.

How was work?

We had an unspoken understanding that we never talked about mine.

Becoming impossible, she said, between mouthfuls. And I realised for the first time, it seemed, that she ate painfully slowly. My plate was almost empty, as was Jenny's.

Like everything else, she continued.

What's impossible, Mummy? Jenny asked.

We're working on a site, darling, that some people think is sacred.

So you've had more of it, I said.

It seems to now go with the territory. Baghdad, and now here. Who would have thought that archaeology and politics could make such a combustible mix?

Combustible, Jenny repeated, as if she was savouring the word.

There are misunderstandings, darling. About the present and the past. And they can lead to demonstrations. People throwing things.

Pussy Riot, Jenny said.

Sarah gave me a concerned-parent look.

One of them jumped on the bonnet of the car. And I asked Daddy for a coloured what's-it-called.

Balaclava, I said. And don't worry. It was all quite uneventful.

The smell of fish permeated the house afterwards. I put Jenny to bed and she wrinkled her nose, as if to dispel it. I entered the office where Sarah was working and found it hanging round there too, like some ghostly residue. She asked what the fish was and I told her it was a zander, some odd Mitteleuropean cross between a pike and a perch.

You hated it, I said. She had her glasses on and was going through some notes.

No, she said, it was quite lovely, but boy does it stink the place.

And I wondered did we have extractor fans.

No, she said. Open the doors and the windows.

So I opened them all, but the smell persisted, intermingled with the humidity of the suburban fumes.

We may have to leave soon, she said. It's becoming intolerable.

And I didn't ask what was becoming intolerable. It was a broad subset that covered many different things.

Where would we go?

England, I suppose.

I'll have no work there.

Aren't there people to be followed? An errant wife or a wayward husband? Don't they counterfeit Gucci bags there?

And what about you?

I'm worried about Jenny. And I'm in need of a – what do they call it? A sabbatical.

It began to rain later, one of those sudden heavy downpours that seem to come from a solid lake above the skies. And I realised every door and window was open, water was trickling in on the carpets and the window sashes, and I went around the house once more, systematically closing them. I went back to bed then, and curled my arms around her.

I feel I'm drowning, she said, only half-awake.

It's the rain, I said. I've closed all the windows.

No, she said. I feel I'm drowning, in you.

31

How long, I asked Istvan, do we have to wait for an appointment to visit the city morgue?

It is the times, he told me. Most of the city works staggered hours. People are talking about blackouts too, which can't be good.

For a morgue? I asked him, and he smiled.

Morgue will have its own generator. Meanwhile, there are government ministers need protection, paranoid billionaires, party bosses, is good time for security in general.

I didn't get the connection, but let it go.

I am making list, expanded list of possible clients. In times like these, protectors need protection.

Protectors of what?

Government buildings, power plants, TV stations. You are well acquainted with war zones?

He knew that I was.

Security is stretched, private enterprise fills the gap.

Is this a war zone?

Not yet. But we — how you say — live in hope. Work for everybody.

I had to admire his quite insane optimism.

Besides, he said, you have appointment.

And I had, I remembered. With our bushy-eyebrowed therapist. So I walked back out on to those hot, deceptive streets. If I was to believe him, this sweet, baking tranquillity was just a crust that hid a boiling magma of volcanic chaos, just about to erupt. But I couldn't quite make the leap. Boomboxes and transgendered protest do not a revolution make. At least not traditionally. And when I made it to the Viennese's office, Sarah was already sitting at her chosen spot by the open window.

She dove right in.

I received a call, she told us, and thought I had better discuss it here rather than in that alpine house we rented, in the bedroom, in the kitchen, in that glassy place they call the bathroom. In the car, even. Our domestic circumstances, I couldn't call them fraught, doctor – are you a doctor by the way? No? Sweet Jesus, why not? Well our domestic circumstances aren't what you would call fraught, since so little comes to the surface, so little is spoken. We're walking on what we both know is thin ice and how I hate that phrase, doctor, why do we need metaphors, anyway? The ice is thin; it covers a lake or a river and is about to crack and the walkers sink in and maybe drown and that's the metaphor, isn't it? But it's a bad one, doctor, because if the ice is thin and about to crack, it's not from any pressure from above, but the volcanic possibilities below, about to erupt, and another metaphor, I'm mixing them but they only work if you mix them. Anyway, I thought I'd discuss it here rather than in that brittle ice palace we live in, but that doesn't work either, doctor, it's nothing to do with ice, it's the heat that gets me, the humidity, it seems to be presaging a thunderclap or a lightning strike, or if nothing as dramatic as that, definitely a migraine. Yes, I get headaches in the heat, doctor, and lately more of them when at home. And you ask again, did I get a call, yes I did, I got a call and halfway through the call I remembered something I had noticed but never allowed myself become aware of, if you know what I mean, I had noticed it but filed it away under troubling, to be dealt with later. My husband hasn't been wearing his ring of late, and the call brought it all into perspective, gave me, if not an explanation, at least a reason. Who called, Jonathan? Visa called, that's who. They wanted to check a rather large purchase from a jeweller's. And at first I had a tiny flutter around what I still persist in thinking of as the heart. Yes, my heart positively leapt, Jonathan, at the thought that you might have bought me a gift. But then they had to spoil it all and mention the date, and I realised that whomever it was bought for, it was not bought for me. He cooked a fish on that day, doctor, and I remember that because it was unusual, a gesture of some weird scaly kind, so I received a portion of baked zander, I think he called it, and someone else received a bracelet of – what were they, darling? Pearls, of course, you always bought the best gifts, I remember that, your taste was immediate and generally impeccable, you had that talent for surprise that used to take my breath away. So there must be someone else out there who's deserving of a trinket that cost two hundred and fifty dollars, a number which must become astronomical in that currency you use here. And they are hard to handle, I will admit that, and maybe Jonathan didn't have enough of them, couldn't make his way to the hole in the wall to get a wad of those smudgy, sweaty bills. Or maybe she was with him at the time, the deserving one let's call her, so he was foolish enough to use his plastic, forgetting that at the very least a bill would arrive at the home of the undeserving one, and in the worst-case scenario, a phone call. That's how it works, doctor, I remember it well, in the first flush of what's-it-called – romance, maybe – you forget all sorts of things. So I was in the kitchen at the time, doctor, and Jenny was finishing her cereal and the heat, my God the heat, it was hardly nine o'clock and my brain was already beginning to congeal, so I dealt with it, doctor, I was rather proud of my demeanour, I am getting good, I told myself, at dealing with things, so I drove Jenny to her school – and it was only on the drive, through those god-awful fields with the nondescript towns whose names I can never remember, the air conditioning had time to work and the humidity reached a level that was bearable, it was only then – I was passing a big grain elevator and a system of overhead pipes that seemed to go on for ever – that the full import of the call sank in. I tried to think of explanations – had he bought it for me and subsequently lost it? – had it been stolen? – was there a significant date coming up? – my birthday is in February, doctor, and our anniversary in May – was he keeping the gift in abeyance, so to speak? – but I know my husband, doctor, when he surprises you he does it immediately, he is an immediate sort of man – and none of the explanations, doctor, could cover what I knew to be the dismal truth – that he had bought it for and given it to the deserving one. Has she a name, Jonathan? She must, but I don't want to know it. And then over the fields of that yellow stuff they grow here – what's it called? Rape? – I could see the line of police and the protesters already in place and I could hear the chant already – I'm on a dig, doctor, of a site that's causing some controversy – and I thought I can't go on with this for very much longer, I need an out, an exit, there was a reason we three came here, but I'm finding it very hard to remember what it was . . .

She left then, and we both sat there. His eyebrows were furrowed and silent for once. I almost felt sorry for him, his predicament, his chosen profession, the patience one would need for it, the mental endurance. There was a fly buzzing in the room and the sound of traffic through the open window.

I bought it for her, I explained.

Ah. Well, that's hopeful. And you mislaid it?

No. A woman took it. She presumed it was hers.

Ah. That's not hopeful. Not hopeful at all.

He sighed, regretfully, I thought. And remember being surprised that he felt so much for us.

She has a name?

I don't know it.

There is or has been a relationship? An intimacy?

Of course.

The plot thickens.

Yes, I said. That's what plots do. Like gravy.

Gravy?

It thickens. Or one thickens it.

You thickened it?

The plot? Yes, perhaps I did. It was interesting what she said about metaphor, doctor. How we can't live without it.

Can't we?

Live without – even that's a metaphor, isn't it? We won't die without it, but we can't explain ourselves, anything about us, without it.

And the metaphor here is?

A plot that thickens. Like gravy before cooking. But it never thickens of its own accord. It is thickened, doctor, by whoever cooks. And she was right, you know. With her cooking metaphor. I bought her pearls. But I gave her a zander.

A zander? he asked.

A pike-perch.

And, he said, you thickened the thing – deliberately – yourself—

Accidentally, doctor. I saved a woman from drowning.

Admirable.

At the beginning, perhaps.

And now you are stuck, so to speak, in the gravy.

More like treacle, doctor.

I do not know treacle.

A cloying, sugary substance that tends to stick to whatever it encounters.

Treacle, then. Another metaphor.

We can't do without them, it seems.

And her? Can you do without her?

I am definitely willing to try.

163

32

I found a café with a humidifier that reached the street tables. I sat there, waiting for a waitress, but none came. I took out a notepad then and began to write. I wrote one version of a goodbye, but the veil of atomised spray fell on the pages and smudged them, the way tears would. And I thought, how strange, the circling nozzle attached to the wall below the sunshade is supplying all of the emotion. Surely some of it should come from me. So I tore out the page and wrote again. I shielded the fresh page with the tearful one and managed to write an unsmudged letter of goodbye.

It was almost dark by the time I was done. So for some reason I knew there would be no cello sounding out, doing its baroque thing around the cobbled streets. Something had to finish, I knew, and I had heard enough of it, for the time being at least. But everything else was much the same. The tiled arch in the fading light, the antique courtyard, the bullet-grey stone steps fanning upwards into the shadows. There was an outline behind the lace curtain of the apartment next to hers and I imagined the neighbour's face with its dispassionate stare. I found the door unlocked when I pushed it and it swung slowly open. It had done so before to the accompaniment of the cello suites, so the little creak it made seemed plaintive and lonely.

I walked inside and it was all there again, the sofa beneath the window, without its cello for once, the curtains blowing softly from the blessed breeze outside, the half-open door to my right with the mattress visible on the floor. I half-expected to see her sleeping there, like the Rokeby Venus, face turned away from me. But there were only rumpled sheets visible, and there were no garments thrown about the floor. I folded the note, but the unwritten side of paper seemed to be crying out for a name. I didn't know her name, so I addressed it simply to 'dear'. It seemed as good a name as any for her, so when I had walked inside and whistled a tune and ascertained she was not in the bathroom either, I smoothed the sheets on the mattress, almost longingly, and left the note on top of them. I walked outside then and pulled the door behind me, careful not to let it make that final click. She might have forgotten her keys, I thought, and as I made my way down the stairs, it gradually began to build. A constriction in my chest, a sense of panic, a sudden sense of loss, as if someone or something had died. So this is how it feels, I thought, to lose somebody and know you won't be able to see them again. What surprised me was the physicality of it, the muscular impact. I could hardly make it down those steps. And I thought everything the scientists tell us is wrong: there is a heart and a soul and it is stronger than this body of mine. And there was a sound now, echoing round the arch, and I realised it was coming from my phone.

It was a relief to hear the voice. Istvan's, as if the real world could take precedence again. And as I walked down the cobbled street on to the boulevard, it all returned, the traffic, the evening heat, the hissing sprays of the humidifiers from the sidewalk cafés.

We have appointment, he said, tomorrow. Eleven thirty.

Where? I asked stupidly. I had to remind myself I had a business.

City morgue, he said. In the twelfth district. For you, me and your friend.

What friend? I asked stupidly, again.

Psychic friend, he said. Who sent us there.

I thanked him and cut off the call. But the moment I had done so, I suddenly missed his voice. Any voice. The feeling had returned, the constriction in my chest, as if a metal hand were closing on it, and the fingers were my ribs. Was that it? I wondered, the last goodbye? And I realised I had nowhere to go, nowhere I wanted to go. Home seemed impossible, for a while at least, and the only place of rest I could think of was that mattress, with my note waiting on the smooth bedsheets, but that seemed impossible too. So I did what all the lost ones do. I walked.

I don't know how long I was walking, but I became aware, and it was an awareness that slowly crept up on me, of someone following. I wasn't used to being followed, I had always been the follower. But I sensed, I couldn't have heard, the slide of canvas sandals on the pavement behind me. I got the scent, then, of a fresh body in a summer dress, fresher than all the dank city air around me, and I knew she was behind me. I slowed, and felt her hand slip through my arm, in that quite unthinking way she had done it the first night we met.

The thing is, she said, it felt so different with you. With us. You were my twin.

I could feel the hand uncurling round my ribs, the constriction lifting, and I could breathe once more. So this is what it feels like, I thought, to find someone again.

Don't talk, she said. I don't want you to talk. I want you to hear what I have to say. You want to forget it all, I understand. You want to forget me, I understand that too. But the thing is, I met you in another life. There's another world, where this never dies. And it has all happened before.

And it had, I knew that somehow. I was walking in another's place.

With who? I asked. And stupidly, I thought of grammar. I should have said 'with whom'.

You know who, she said. He lives on the other side. And you must take me there.

Why? I asked, stupidly again.

Because, she said, and her logic seemed impeccable, I cannot go there alone.

So we walked back down the boulevard of linden trees. There was a strange forbidden frisson to this, a sense of adult abandon. I was with her in public, among the night city crowds. They surged around like moths, past us and away; we were mosquitoes, flitting through them, never touching. We came to that shell of concrete rising out of the pavement and I led her down the steps that he had taken with the gentlest of touches on her elbow. She moved wherever I moved her, like an obedient pet. Down towards the platform, where all the day's heat had gathered into a dark night cloud. We took the metro then and she sat on the wooden seat, laid her head back against the smudged glass and caught my gaze, in an amused, abstract way. There was a transaction here, a goodbye gift, but whether the gift was for her or him I didn't allow myself to dwell on. I knew my capacity for jealousy and knew I had to keep it at bay. The train slowed then and we walked back up the steps and found ourselves on those rising, medieval cobbled streets and I almost didn't recognise them at night. But I could see the shape of the castle in the gloom, a piece of moon dangling above it, and I let it guide me. Through those streets with the crushed windows and the sagging architraves. And I saw the sign then, down the thinnest of streets where the gutters of the roofs above almost touched each other. *Musikinstrumente.*

He runs a music shop, I said.

Of course, she said.

She walked down the street, like someone remembering.

There was a light glowing from the window. I came behind her, and saw the dim gloom of the music shop, the warm glow from the kitchen at the back. And I felt jealous again. Her stillness was unnerving, outside that window. It implied a world of feeling I would never know.

We should go, I said. And she shook her head.

Don't do something foolish. And she shook her head again.

You want me to leave you here?

She nodded.

So I turned and left her there. The street was hers, if anyone's. Definitely not mine.

As I rounded the corner, I heard the crack of splintering glass. Was she the stone-throwing type? I wondered. But I thought it best not to look back.

33

The house was still when I got home. It was late, but I didn't know how late. There was a note on the kitchen table that read: I'm sleeping with Jenny tonight. So this is it, I thought, the new dispensation. I went to open her bedroom door and enjoy for a moment the spectacle of them both curled up together, but I stopped my hand by the door handle and thought better of it. There was a quiet, deathly peace in the house that didn't seem to want disturbing. So I crawled into the empty bed and then began to worry about sleeping. There was a box of pills by the cabinet on her side that read *Stilnoct*. I took one of them, swallowed some water, and when sleep didn't arrive, I took another. And some small death must have taken me over, because when I awoke the sun was pouring through the French windows and they both were gone.

I was already late, I knew, so I drove without breakfast and bought a takeaway coffee from one of those stalls by the river. And I crossed the metal bridge again and saw the barges below draw streams of dirty yellow in their wakes, like urine. As I approached the other side, I could see Gertrude standing by the window on the second floor, something white in her arms, which I assumed to be the Pomeranian. She was looking towards me and I wondered, could she see me from that distance, a tiny figure on this cathedral of rusting steel?

How is he, I asked, after she had buzzed me in, and how is his luxurious patella?

Luxating, she said. And thank you for asking, but Phoebe is a she. And luxating has ceased, entirely.

I took the Polaroid from my pocket and saw the bright, smiling blonde-haired face. Of how many years ago? I wondered.

We have to visit city morgue. Are we to assume she is dead, Jonathan? I'm not sure I could bear such a conclusion.

We assume nothing, I said. You mentioned a small room, that she cannot leave. I visited a brothel, I was wrong. This could turn out to be—

A wild-goosey chase?

And her eyebrows lifted when she said this and I had to smile.

A dead end, I said.

I had texted Sarah to see would she pick up Jenny and she had replied simply, yes. It was monosyllabic, but a reply none the less. Could I assume from that that we were still communicating?

And your wife, Gertrude asked, how is she?

You know my wife? I asked, stupidly, because I knew she didn't.

She was the reason we first met, she said.

Let's forget about Sarah, I said, for the moment.

Sarah, she said. Yes, I remember the name. And she took my arm with one of hers, while the other held the dog.

Shall we?

She moved me towards the door.

The dog, I asked her, do we have to take her?

I am afraid we do, she said. You are afraid we will look stupid?

It's just that pets may not be allowed in city morgues, I said.

In that case, she said, we leave her in the car.

She held my arm in the lift down and the Pomeranian licked my fingers. I could feel her breast beneath the smart summer dress she was wearing, with my elbow.

Time, she said. It moves so slowly, sometimes it almost stops.

Are we in a hurry? I asked her.

No, she said and the old lift creaked. She turned her face to me, and I could discern the beauty that must have been there, some years ago, beneath the make-up.

But it plays tricks on us. Tricks that we never are prepared for. Like here, she said. I lift my face to yours, look at that downy mouth and wonder, have I ever done that before?

Downy? I said. I touched my chin, and remembered that I had shaved.

Your mouth, she said. Turns downwards. You would have been my type, all of those years ago.

How many? I asked.

Ach, you disappoint me, Jonathan. Never ask a woman's age.

I'm sorry, I said. But there was a bubble of flirtation in the lift that was not at all unpleasant. She had those Marlene Dietrich cheekbones, old Gertrude, and that Teutonic mouth, carefully delineated with a make-up pencil. And I realised that the beauty of this frisson with her was that it would never come to anything. So I allowed her to hold my elbow to her breast as the lift doors opened, and we crossed the street to where Istvan was waiting with his car. And perhaps I had a future as a consort to older women if the world I knew fell totally apart.

34

The old glass-fronted sign read *Morga*, and repeated the word in German, *Leichenschauhaus*, but the building hardly needed a sign, because everything about it spelt morgue. It was an old breezeblock structure in the grounds of what once must have been a hospital, but most of the buildings had boarded windows and there were weeds growing in the cracks between the paving stones. Odd, forlorn figures walked around, and there were two lab assistants smoking by a double door covered with strips of thick, industrial plastic. Where the ambulances backed in, I surmised, as Istvan parked the car and we walked towards the drab entrance.

Gertrude held my arm again and cradled her dog with her other hand. We signed forms at the reception through the door and nobody made mention of the canine. A pretty lab assistant in a clean white coat led us past what must have been a pathology room, where two women worked over a marble slab, towards an industrial lift. And as the lift groaned its way downwards, I wondered at how death was so often attended by women. Was that brisk, feminine practicality what was needed to deal with dead bodily tissue? Or maybe our exits and our entrances to this world needed female guidance. By those lights mythology had got it wrong. Charon should have been a woman and the Grim Reaper a uniformed girl.

Anyway, she led us forwards, our pretty white-coated Charon, out of a lift and through a series of subterranean corridors. There was an overpowering smell of formaldehyde. The dog moaned, as if sensing the otherworld.

Hush hush, Phoebe, Gertrude whispered.

We entered two swinging double doors and the temperature had dropped perceptibly. We found ourselves in a long room with fluorescent tubes fixed to the concrete ceiling, throwing a bilious light on a metal wall of trays, each tray with its own number and handle.

The girl murmured to Istvan and he murmured to me.

She asked me, do we want to see them all?

And Gertrude was looking, painfully, at the row of handles.

A small room, said Istvan, that she cannot leave.

How many? I asked.

And the assistant turned her head to me. She understood my English.

Fifteen, she said, currently.

There is no need, whispered Gertrude, who seemed alarmingly fragile, for once.

Hold Phoebe.

She placed the dog in my arms, and it whined in protest.

Give me Petra.

And I eventually understood, she meant the Polaroid. I took it from my pocket with my free hand and placed it in hers. She held it towards that wall of metal.

I could see her hand, her painted nails, the young girl smiling, dangling from them, all of the colour bleached by whatever the years does to acetate. And the Polaroid was trembling slightly, although Gertrude's hand was steady, tense with all the veins showing.

Achh, she whispered, and seemed to glide towards that bank of steel. The Polaroid fluttered as if in its own private breeze. And I wondered what was I to understand about what was going on here.

The faded image of Petra was drawing her towards that metal wall. Or so it would appear. Her feet moved forwards, slowly, her eyes were half-closed, there was that familiar half-smile hovering round her lips. And the young girl held between her finger and thumb stared back at me, flickering in the invisible breeze, as soft as an image on a magic lantern.

There was a row of handles from ceiling to floor. And behind each handle was the emptiness of death, a cadaver awaiting identification, the pale and frozen flesh the spirit leaves.

There was a smell, like plastic burning. The Pomeranian moaned. And I could see the faded colours on the young girl's cheeks turning slowly brown.

This one, said Gertrude, and she stopped by a steel handle. The number said 11.

This is most irregular, the assistant began, but Gertrude cut her off.

I know, she said. And the image was fading on the Polaroid, as if the chemicals had given up the ghost. It flared, like a negative after-image, and became an out-of-focus blur. It curled, as if the impossible had happened, and it was burning.

Little Petra, she whispered. What happened?

She placed the Polaroid in my free hand and I had to blow on my fingers, it felt so hot. She wrapped her painted fingers round the metal handle.

May I? she asked the assistant. And the assistant nodded.

She began to pull the tray.

I stepped to one side, to give her room.

A mist came out, as she pulled the handle back, as if a ghost had exhaled. I told myself it was the refrigeration. But what I saw next told me it wasn't.

I saw a pair of coloured canvas sandals on the horizontal tray. Then a pair of ankles, slim calves, whitened by their spell in this dead refrigerator, but I knew their skin colour had once been sallow, almost dark. I saw a dress then that I recognised and the outline of underwear beneath it that I would have recognised too, because they both had lain on top of mine on the bare floor, when she pointed them out from the mattress and asked, Don't they look good together, our clothes? I saw the hands, which must have been placed across the stomach by some dutiful lab attendant. There was a torn V at the neck of the dress, and part of her frozen breast was exposed. The dark, inert hair curled around her chin and her mouth, which seemed pursed slightly, as if ready to ask a question. A question, perhaps, about this absurd cold metal bed she was lying on.

Her eyes were closed. The same dutiful lab attendant, probably. I thanked him silently for it. Her eyelashes were stiffened with hoarfrost.

How long has she been here? I asked, though my voice seemed too loud, even to me. There was a hush in this moment that was beyond speech.

The assistant turned her canvas shoe sideways, and I saw an identification tag attached to the strap.

Close to three weeks now.

Where was she found?

Floating in the river.

A suicide? I asked.

Most likely. No one has claimed the body.

You get them all the time? asked Istvan. His voice was matter-of-fact, as if he had seen nothing out of the ordinary. And for once I wished I could be like him.

Every now and then.

Autopsy?

If one is requested.

We think we know who this girl is. Right, Jonathan?

Yes, I said. Perhaps we do.

Petra, he said. And he checked the screen on his phone. Pavel.

And I excused myself. I said I needed some air.

I stood out by the plastic strips where the lab assistants had been smoking. I tried to breathe, slowly. I heard the clack of heels on the dull cement then and saw that Gertrude had followed me. She had a cigarette packet in her hand, with one already dangling from her mouth.

You want one?

I don't smoke.

There is a time for everything.

And she placed one in my mouth, took a lighter from her pack and flicked the little wheel.

Tell me, she said, as the cigarette burned and the unfamiliar smoke filled my lungs.

I know that girl, I said.

How could you? she asked.

I don't know, I said. I pulled her from the river.

You saved her?

In a manner of speaking.

And now she's dead.

Maybe she was dead then.

You really mean that?

You told me, some time ago, there was something dying inside me.

Something dead.

Maybe you meant her.

Maybe.

Can you make sense of it for me?

She looked at me and exhaled slowly, through those carefully painted lips. A small stream of grey smoke came with her breath.

Some things don't make sense, Jonathan.

She separated the syllables.

One long and two short.

35

We drove back along the brown river with three different kinds of silences between us. Istvan's was practical, regretful, and his face above the steering wheel had settled into a solemn mask, the mask of someone who is used to death and knows how to deal with it. Gertrude was shrouded in electronic smoke in the back seat, which created a halo around her immobile silhouette. I simply said nothing.

Istvan broke it, eventually.

We must inform the parents, no?

Of course, I murmured.

Will you do that or will I?

You have their details? I asked. Give them to me and I'll call them.

You knew? Istvan looked at Gertrude through the rear-view mirror.

Knew what?

That she was dead? In that small room that she could not leave?

I'm sure all three of us suspected. Even the parents.

But it's your job to know, isn't it? All about the dead?

My job is to hold palms, close my eyes, tell people what they want to hear.

But you told him about the room? The small room.

Is just some nonsense I spouted. Came into my head.

So you're not what they would call psychic, then?

No. There is another word for me. Charlatan.

And she blew the smoke away, waved it from her face with her hand.

Let me out here.

You want to walk?

I have to.

I could see the bridge with the stone angels looming up ahead of us, when he stopped the car. And I felt the need to walk as well.

Let me out here, I told Istvan, and he nodded, as if he understood.

We all need some air, he said. I drive back to office, call the parents?

No, I said. Let me do that.

She was walking by the parapet, and I could see the tourist boats beyond her in the river below. As the car passed me, I drew alongside her. She bent down to the Pomeranian, fixing a small lead to the collar round its neck.

I think Phoebe needs to walk, too.

And we both walked then, slowed to a crawl by the tiny scraping feet of the dog.

You want me to make sense of it for you? I can't. But all I will tell you is, you are a good detective.

Am I?

Parents asked you to find the girl? You found her. Long before you knew it.

I met her there.

I pointed towards the huge but oddly delicate hawsers of the suspension bridge.

On the bridge?

She had climbed beyond the protective wire. She was in the shadow of the statue of the angel.

And what? You thought she was about to jump? You stopped her.

I tried. She jumped anyway. Then I jumped after.

Was your first mistake.

Why do you say that?

I don't know. Just a feeling.

And my second?

I don't want to know either. Can only imagine.

Come, let me show you.

And so I retraced our wet steps, from the river to the small cobbled streets, to the arch, with its almost Moorish tiles, where there was no cello playing.

I walked home with her, through here.

Again I must ask, why?

I told myself I was worried. That she needed a hospital.

You told yourself.

Yes.

We walked through the arch and entered the small, fanciful courtyard.

And then?

We walked up those steps, to her rooms.

Her rooms.

She played the cello. She told me she was on sabbatical from the orchestra.

And?

Every time I walked back past, I heard the cello playing.

You hear it now?

I shook my head. I walked towards the steps, which fanned upwards towards the shadows.

Don't ask me to go up there.

Why not?

Some things I should not know.

She took two steps backwards, into the shadow of the arch. Her legs, with their elegant shoes, stayed in the bright sunlight. She had kept herself well, I remember thinking.

You stepped out of time, no? You did that thing that lovers do. There was no beginning or end. You had met each other in another life.

How did you know?

And she smiled at that.

I was young once.

But she didn't exist. She was dead.

The loved one never does. We create them, out of some damnable need. And when I think back now, I pity the ones I did it with. I would have torn them to shreds and put them back together again to fit the thing I wanted.

And you, Jonathan, she said, you would have been my type. All those years ago.

How many? I asked again. And she had the grace to smile.

Never ask a woman's age. Jo-na-than.

And she turned, walked back into the arch, towards the hot band of sunlight outside it.

Do I need help? I called after her.

But she mustn't have heard. Or if she did, she didn't want to answer.

I did need help, but I walked up those stairs again, alone. I heard my footsteps echo round the curving walls. The shadows above me seemed darker than before and I heard the sharp scratch of a curtain, pulled. It was the neighbouring woman, I saw, with the dark hair behind the lace and I suddenly understood her trepidation. I would have knocked on her door, but I knew now why not to do so. Any questions of mine would have frightened her. And I felt something deeper than fear, like a piece of ice in my stomach.

The door was barely ajar, the way it always had been. I pushed it gently, and heard the familiar creak. I managed to walk inside then and saw the room, bathed in the sunlight from the window. There was a sofa there, with no cello perched upon it. And maybe there had never been a cello. I opened the door to the small kitchen and there was a dryer there, the orbed glass covered in a fine dust. I knelt down and rubbed my finger off the dust, which must have been several weeks old. There was a pink dress inside, lying like a dead thing at the bottom curve of the stainless-steel tumbler. I thought I saw a face then, distorted in the glass, and jumped backwards, slamming my head against the kitchen door.

I must have been stunned for a moment, because I heard the dryer begin to whirr. I shook my head and rubbed my eyes, and it was whirring, manically, then shaking on the bare boards of the kitchen floor, the way unbalanced dryers do. I must have hit a button when I wiped the glass, I thought, and began to press them at random, the wide, worn plastic things, and its whirring grew faster, until I must have hit the right combination, and it gradually began to wind down.

What explanations did I need, I wondered, watching the pink dress float lazily in the last rotations of the tumbler. Maybe I came in alone, wet from the river, maybe I had found this place, this empty hell or heaven. Maybe I had drowned. Maybe I was dead.

I managed to stand and pulled at the kitchen door. It didn't open for a moment; I had to pull it hard enough to splinter the wood, and there was the room outside again, with the sofa, curved like an enormous reclining nude.

I had touched the dead, I thought, or imagined I had, and there was the smell of soft, loamy clay in the room. I forced myself to walk through it, and looked right into the bedroom.

There was the mattress on the bare boards, with my envelope lying on the sheets. Someone had opened it. And that smell was everywhere now; was it sweat or was it clay or was it something much more intimate, an intimacy that was impossible because the other one was dead? I tried to walk into that room, but couldn't make it. I saw the crumpled paper I had written on, with my handwriting, the scribbled word: 'dear'.

36

I was cold, walking back through that arch, through the small cobbled streets on to the hot boulevard with its crowds and its traffic and its humidifying sprays. How easy it was, I found, to remove oneself, to feel barely alive, just a splash of shadow walking through these sunlit passers-by. A boy on a skateboard bumped me and I was glad I could feel it; it reminded me that I had presence, was a physical fact, like all these others, surging around me.

I was a good detective, Gertrude had told me, and I turned that phrase over in my mind, as if it could have brought me some relief. There should be some satisfaction in a job well done, concluded, a case closed, but in this case there was none. I had fulfilled my task without knowing it. The small room she couldn't leave was a morgue refrigerator and she had lain dead inside it on that cold tray for the past three weeks. I could feel a tingling, like that hoarfrost on her eyelashes, all over my skin. I passed the jeweller's and saw the squat grey wedding cake of the opera house on the other side. I walked across the street towards it for no other reason than that it seemed familiar, part of a common landscape that could never have been or a memory that shouldn't exist. I could hear music from inside, and paid the entry fee to the attendant, although she told me that there was a rehearsal in progress, and that tourists could only access the upper levels. It sounded like an overture and I thought I heard a phrase from what she had played from *Rigoletto* as I ascended that huge staircase with its profusion of cherubs and nymphs. There was a group of elderly Japanese tourists staring upwards, holding wireless headsets to their ears as the mysteries of the past were explained to them in a language of their choice, and I mounted the steps past them, to a large, extravagantly mirrored foyer at the very top. I could see my pale face, multiplied everywhere in different directions, brocaded by the red satin curtains wherever I looked. The sound of the orchestra came from somewhere off, a cascading Italian dance that was joined by the distant voice of a tenor. I opened a mirrored door and found myself in what must have been the gods, rows of hard wooden seats, behind a curved balcony with a vertiginous view of the stage far below, and the orchestra pit.

I could see his thinning hair from up above, and the cello between his knees. She had called him Grigory, I remembered. There was a woman next to him, dark hair cascading over her bowing hand, and for a moment I thought that everything else had been a dream – Gertrude, the parents, Petra, the visit to the morgue – and that her sabbatical had finally ended and she was back playing here. Then she bent her head sideways, to turn the pages of the score, and I saw the pair of horn-rimmed glasses the cellist wore, and the matronly bosom, and realised there was no relief, that I was wrong about that too.

So I did what one does when all else fails. I went back to work. Istvan sat at his desk with the fan balanced precariously on the ledge of the open window. He seemed as bothered by the heat as I was by the cold.

I saved you the trouble, he said. I called them.

The parents?

Yes, he nodded. Better to hear it in their own language. The mother wept and I did my best to – how you say it?

Commiserate? I hazarded, and he nodded once again.

But at least they will have what they long for. In those American cop shows.

And what is that?

Closure, he said. Is that not the word? They always need it, before the drama can end, the advertisements come up.

But what if there can be no closure? I asked him softly.

Always is. Otherwise no commercial break.

So, we were in a drama, I thought. Of someone else's devising. Maybe that would explain the arbitrary rules.

They will need an autopsy, I said.

I have asked for one, he said. For dental records, however sad that might seem.

You asked them gently?

Istvan always asks gently, he said in his blunt way.

It was dark when I left and there was not so much rain as mist falling. Mist doesn't fall, I thought, so maybe it was precipitation coming from the river. A kind of summer fog.

I had parked the car across the river so I walked over the bridge again and I looked up at the streetlight gleaming on the wet stone curve of the angel's wing and there she was.

Her back to me, behind the wire mesh that divided the parapet from the walkway. And I wondered how I had climbed it, three weeks ago. It seemed impossible. Maybe I hadn't.

The angel is like you, it cannot see.

She let her hair fall over her eyes as if she didn't want to see either.

And I know, she said, you want to end it all. I know you have a wife waiting in that small shop beneath the castle. But I will have my say before I go. You taught me many things, and I enjoyed all of them but one. You taught me what timbre should be, how to soften and slow my vibrato, you taught me that in the cello suites there is everything one needs to learn about the instrument. And so I learned them all and played them and will keep playing them if there is anything for me where I am about to go. When you start something the way you did, when you make promises the way you did, you have to realise it never ends. I have a child now that can't be born so I'm an unfinished thing, the way those angels are unfinished things. You taught me that too. The man forgot to make the eyes.

She was talking to someone else, I realised. To the first cellist in the opera orchestra.

And she turned to me, from the parapet, where I had met her first, three weeks ago. I could feel her brown eyes looking through me.

Stupid historical fact, she said. And she jumped.

I watched her fall, her coloured canvas sandals leading the way, and she vanished into the mist that obscured the brown river. But I did hear a distant splash.

Yesterday, upon the stair,
I met a man who wasn't there.
He wasn't there again today,
I wish, I wish he'd go away.

Jenny would have loved those verses, I thought. But I dearly hoped she would never learn them.

I heard sudden footsteps on the bridge. But with the mist around, I could see nothing other than the huge hawsers and the steel ropes that clung to them, vanishing into a blur. Then out of the haze I saw three coloured balaclavas running towards me, with bright pastel-yellow dresses beneath them. Black Doc Marten boots and coloured tights. Their dark mouths were open in a scream of panic and I ducked sideways to avoid them. Then behind them came a group of youths in military fatigues, bits of broken metal in their hands, black balaclavas on their bellowing heads.

There was no mistaking the sex of these ones. They were male and they were on punishing business. But the coloured ones had vanished like a wisp, almost the way the girl had vanished, and there was no catching them now.

As the sound of the riot echoed about me, I looked down at the water. The mist was clearing and I wondered would I see her, drifting or floundering her way to the cement bank. I had heard a splash, after all. But I saw nothing.

So I walked on. Faces loomed out of the mist, towards me and away, like ghosts. And that's what ghosts should do, I thought, they should appear and disappear and not cling to the living. I had taken the job, I had found her before her time, but I had found her after all and, whatever else had happened, the job was done.

37

I arrived back to a home that was apparently normal. The mist still hung about, heightening the fairy-tale fantasy of the place. The carved gargoyles on the wooden gate opened obediently and the garden looked just like a garden should, in its umbrella of soft moisture. Jenny was being prepared for bed and Sarah kissed me briskly on my entrance, the way a busy wife would. I made my apologies for being late and took our daughter from her arms, to perform the bedtime rituals.

Come on then, I murmured, I'll read you that story.

Not the Johnny McGory one, please, she said.

Will I begin it?

No, she said. Read me a proper one.

I looked back at Sarah as I turned into the bathroom and hoped to be graced with at least the pretence of a smile. But she looked at me mournfully, and simply appeared lost.

The story in her book was about a giant who didn't want to frighten people but couldn't help doing so, such were the stereotypical clichés attached to giants. People demanded all of the tropes of ogredom from him, and fully expected to run and scream, and willingly did so, but this poor giant had a heart of soft toffee and all he really wanted to do was hug people and be friendly.

I read it dutifully and as I read I began to long for the pitiless morality of the traditional fairy tale, where evil was evil and was never explained, and good was good, as it always had been. But Jenny seemed to love this witless post-modern spin, and had half-closed her eyes before the story ended. So I was kissing her cheek and turning off the light, when she murmured something that stopped me dead in my tracks, the way an old Brothers Grimm fairy tale would have done.

I have a new friend, she said.

So, I said, you have three of them now?

Four, she said. Rebecca, Jessica, Melanie and Petra.

Petra? I echoed. And it felt like an echo. The name, and my voice.

Yes, she said. Petra. And she plays the thing.

What thing?

The cello thing.

A little girl could never play a thing as big as that.

And I was saying anything to take my mind off the chill that seemed to have descended on the room.

Well, she's not always little. Sometimes she's big.

So there's little Petra and big Petra.

Yes. And little Petra has blonde hair and plays the violin like me. And when she's big she plays the other thing. The cello.

Go to sleep, honey. Don't think about such things.

Such things, she murmured. But I have to think about them. Because she's going to teach me.

Teach you what?

The suites.

What suites?

The cello suites. By that man that Mummy likes.

You mean Bach?

Yes, that's his name. Bach.

And she closed her eyes fully, and seemed instantly to be asleep.

She related it all with the simple directness of a child relating a fairy tale. And maybe it was a fairy tale that we had both blundered into. We had been walking, the two of us, and wandered into a Ruritanian wood. And as I walked back from her bedroom to the kitchen and an encounter that I now dreaded, was it my imagination or did the shadows seem blacker, the contrasts between them and the reddish lamplight etched in ink?

Sarah was sitting, pouring water on to a green-tea sachet.

Do you want one? she asked.

Please, I said. And she used the time it took for the kettle to boil again to relish the silence.

Should we divorce? she asked me.

Is that the only option? I replied. And it was hardly a question. It was a statement that hung in the air, like invisible smoke.

Well, she said. We both seem to have made a mess of things.

And is it the kind of mess that ends in divorce?

It is the conventional option, she told me. Isn't that what one does?

One, I thought. I could never think of her as one.

You would never survive it, I said, stupidly.

You mean life without you? I had a life without you once. It was at least coherent.

I thought of the razor wire and the burning tyres and the dull crumping sound of another car bomb and wondered what was coherent about that. But she had been always oddly composed, and I suppose, coherent, in that burning world.

And this isn't?

No, she said. This has become an incoherent mess.

Maybe life, I murmured, is an incoherent mess.

Do you love this woman? she asked.

There was no answer to that question. But I gave the only one that had a hope of being understood.

She's dead, I said.

Oh God, she said. Please. What have you got us into?

She killed herself. She jumped from one of those bridges.

Oh Jonathan.

And with one of those sudden reversals that reminded me why I loved her, she clutched at my hand.

Oh God, she said, as if she knew something I didn't. I really don't want this.

Neither do I, I said.

So, I suppose you have to tell me.

I left a note. After we had that – conversation – about the Visa bill and the bracelet.

Was that a conversation?

It was more like a monologue.

What did the note say?

This is hard, Sarah.

I don't mean the actual words.

It said I wouldn't see her again. And I needed the brace-let back.

She went quiet for a moment. And I could hear the precipitation, dripping from the eaves outside.

You thought so much of me?

Of us, I told her.

She turned her back to me. And all I could look at was that curve where her neck met her shoulder, outlined in yellow by the lamp behind.

Do I need to know the rest? she asked.

I can't explain it, I said.

Could you try?

And I realised, as I was speaking, what a mutable thing truth was. She killed herself, I told her, she climbed above the parapet of the bridge up to the stone foot of the statue and jumped. Her body was pulled from the river and remains on a refrigerated tray in the morgue in the twelfth district, awaiting identification.

Because of what you wrote?

How could I know?

I don't know. How can one know anything?

And she was right, of course. How could I be certain I was here, talking to the woman who was still my wife?

There was a man she was upset about. A cellist, in the opera.

A cellist, in the opera.

She put her cup down on the metal tray above the sink and turned and came towards me. She put her arms around me, but I could sense the stiffness, the reluctance in her limbs.

Do I need to know more, Jonathan?

I hope not, I said.

Because I'm going to bed now. I'm shaking on the inside.

Not on the outside?

You know Sarah never shakes on the outside.

And she didn't. That was her coherence. She was always calm, searching through the rubble with her elasticated gloves, no matter what the chaos was outside.

I should ask you to sleep in the other room. But I don't know how to. And I don't know why I don't.

That's all right, I said.

No, it's not all right. Maybe it will never be all right.

And she turned away from me and walked towards the bedroom.

Every word I had told her was the truth, yet every word was a lie. How could that be? I wondered, like a child, trying to understand the rules of logic. Had I left out the essentials for my own convenience, to retain some final value in her estimation, or because I couldn't understand them myself? It was the truth: I had met her, allowed her to take the bracelet, written her a note and found out that she had died. And yet it was the most profound untruth I could have spoken.

I saw a whisky bottle sitting among the cartons of cereal above the fridge. I poured myself a glass, broke out some ice and sat by the hard wood of the kitchen table, savouring the burning taste of it. It would be good, I thought, to drink it down, to reach that place where the inside impinged on the outside and nothing needed to be certain any more. Drunkenness. I remembered the state, but whenever I had allowed myself to get there it had been out of an excess of excitement, abandon, happiness even. I had never got drunk deliberately, to blur the lines that should have been separate because one couldn't understand them any more. And I wasn't about to now. I was a rational being, I told myself, I dealt in puzzles that had solutions and sometimes they ended in death, but death was death, that final and unreachable place beyond where thinking lay, where all of the puzzles ended. And it provided – what was that word Istvan used, so beloved of the television serials? Closure. A corpse provided its own full stop.

So I finished the glass and walked quietly into the bedroom we shared. She seemed to be asleep, or maybe she lay curled in the posture of hope, hope that sleep might yet arrive. I laid my clothes on the floor beneath my side and crept beneath the sheets, with as little disturbance as possible.

The whisky must have done its job because I fell immediately asleep. And was it the whisky that woke me two or three hours later, or the wind, opening those French windows? I could not be sure. But I woke, anyway, quite suddenly and the curtains were blowing in the soft breeze from outside and it was still raining on the lawns and she was in the room.

I wake up, she was saying, and I don't know where I am, and my hair is wet and I don't know why and then I remember what you said and I know that you have left me. And I feel dead again and there is mud in my mouth and I can't talk. And I remember then that you have a wife and a daughter and that it is impossible and blah blah blah all those things, but I am back on the bridge waiting for you and there is something living inside me, a little one that I could maybe teach some day, all of the things you taught me, the way to make the instrument sing, the way to play not just the notes but the spirit of the notes. And there is something left, you see, even though it's over like you say and I'm left in this dead place, there is something left that will get us back to where we were and where everything is alive again.

She was talking to someone else, not to me. And maybe that was the last part of the puzzle. She had always been talking to someone else and not to me. And I felt grief-stricken suddenly, for reasons I knew I would never understand. I had to be jealous now, about what a woman who was dead felt for a man I had never known. And Sarah shifted in the bed beside me and asked, still half-asleep, what was that breeze that was blowing, had someone opened the windows, and I kissed the back of her head and said the wind must have opened them and I turned, and she was gone, there was just the curtains blowing and soft rain still falling, mercifully, outside.

I got out of the bed and padded quietly over the bare floorboards across the space she had occupied and looked through the French windows at the dripping linden trees. It was still humid and hot outside, with that fine mist everywhere and the soft drops falling from every leaf and branch. I could never have been certain she had even been here, I thought, and then I heard the sound that told me that she had.

It was a cello, playing quietly but confidently, from a room inside, the first prelude of the first suite, and by now I knew it so well that it seemed natural, even right, that it was coming from somewhere in the house we lived in.

You've left the CD on, haven't you? Sarah asked.

And I lied again.

Yes, I said. I'm sorry.

And the fact that I was sorry was the truth.

Well, turn it off, please. I need to sleep.

And I moved to the bedroom door to turn off what I didn't know how to turn off when suddenly it stopped. And Jenny was standing in the doorway in those pyjamas she wore with the imprints of small elephants.

She was playing, she said, still delightfully sleepy but strangely matter-of-fact. I told her not to play the thing when everyone's asleep.

What thing? I asked, and I wondered why I was asking when I already knew.

The thing. That rhymes with yellow.

Cello? said Sarah.

Yes, Jenny said. The cello.

Who plays the cello? Sarah asked. Her voice had reduced itself to a whisper.

My new friend, Jenny said.

And what's your new friend's name?

Don't, I whispered to Sarah.

Daddy knows her name. Petra.

I reached out to touch Sarah's hand. But she drew hers away, as if stung by a wasp.

Mummy will take you to bed now, love, she said, as softly as she could.

Please, Jenny said, and stretched out her arms as Sarah walked towards her.

And Mummy will sleep with you tonight, in case you get frightened.

Why would I be frightened?

The plain way she asked this question was frightening enough.

38

We both drove her to school the next day, in Sarah's car.

You will tell me, Sarah said as Jenny walked towards the monumental steps with her coloured schoolbag bobbing on her shoulder, what is going on and if it doesn't make sense, I'll book the next flight home.

I don't know what's going on, I said.

You never lied to me before, she said.

And I'm not lying now.

You took our daughter to meet that girl.

I didn't.

How else would she know her name?

She has imaginary friends, I said. Could you explain that?

This is different, Jonathan, she said. There's something in our house, in our family that wasn't there before.

Like those cufflinks, I said, and immediately regretted it.

Fuck you, she said, fuck you, fuck you, fuck you. Maybe the next time we talk should be with that therapist. And maybe you should walk from here.

*   *   *

I did, and it was a relief to walk. I walked through the crumbling suburbs beyond the grand boulevards to the forlorn end of the river where it ran off into those small canals. I called Istvan on the way and he picked me up by an empty skatepark and drove me to the morgue, where the body of Petra was lying in the small room that she couldn't leave

The parents, if they were hers, were already waiting underneath the old glassy sign. Istvan wrote in the book and we descended again, with the pretty lab assistant with the rubber gloves, in the industrial lift down to the chilling depths where the refrigerators hummed

The mother wept quietly when she saw the row of metal handles and the father wiped his eyes when the tray was pulled out. That is the way grief happens, I remember thinking, quietly and without much fuss.

Petra, the mother whispered, when the body was revealed. It was unchanged and looked like it always would be. The small fringe of hoarfrost round the eyelids.

Ask her how can she be sure, I said to Istvan and he repeated the question.

Mladez, she said, or something like it. She walked forwards and pulled the sad frozen dress to reveal the knee. There was a birthmark there, and I wondered how I had never noticed it before.

Unde, she said.

Dove, said Istvan. Dove, they used to call it.

I could distinguish something like the blur of wings and a tiny birdlike body. For some reason I felt the tears now, flowing down my face. And for some reason I was embarrassed and I turned away.

The lab assistant snapped her gloves softly. Out of discomfort, I supposed. We were all of us, suddenly, uninvited guests at a funeral.

We should give them some . . . how do you say?

Space? I said to Istvan.

Yes, he said, almost proudly. For moment of closure.

Outside, we stood by the discoloured strips of industrial plastic that covered the ambulance bay.

Will there be an autopsy now?

Only if they request it.

He took off his jacket and folded it with two meaty hands. I saw the sweat marks underneath the armpits and had to remind myself that it was hot.

What about bill? he asked.

Don't bill them, I said.

We have many expenses. Phone, petrol, time.

Put them all against me, I said.

For what reason? he asked. They are clients, like any other.

For reasons of closure, I told him.

And I realised I needed whatever that inadequate word meant, desperately. I needed the credits to roll and the commercials to begin.

Her parents walked out, blinking in the bright summer air, like two bewildered penguins. They stood then on the cracked cement path and moved from one patch of weed to the other and I realised that, like most of the lost souls I had seen wandering here, they weren't sure where to go.

How did they get here? I asked Istvan.

By train, I suppose. And then by foot.

Will you give them a lift?

What about you?

I can walk, I told him.

So I watched him walk over to them. I saw rather than heard the conversation, the nodding, the bowing, the clutching of hands, and after he had helped them into the back and the car had sputtered off, I saw the lab assistant emerging through the strips of plastic to smoke a cigarette.

She gestured the packet towards me, mutely, in her plastic-covered hand and I took one, for lack of something else to do.

Is sad, she said.

Yes, I nodded.

But we never know the story. We don't need to know the story. We deal with cadaver, organ, cause of death. Is bad to know the story.

Is it?

Yes, she said. Better to stay uninvolved.

Can I see her again? I asked.

The corpse?

She smiled bitterly and blew smoke out of her delicious mouth.

You knew her?

I shook my head. And it was true; how could I have known her?

I was hired to find her.

Like policeman? she questioned. Detective?

She walked me back through the strips of plastic into the empty ambulance bay and down a set of grey stairs. She snapped her gloves once more and smiled at me before she pulled open the great steel doors.

Is most irregular, she said.

Perhaps, I said. But I just need five minutes.

Tray number eleven, she said. You can open yourself?

I heard the doors close softly behind me as I walked forwards. She was giving me privacy, and I wasn't sure I welcomed it. But I pulled back the handle on the tray and saw the coloured sandals again, the stiff dress edged up above the knee where the birthmark I had never known about was evident. *Unde.*

And now it looked nothing like a dove. Just a smudge, slightly darker than the rest of the skin. I reached out a finger and touched it and for some reason was surprised by the cold, dead feel.

I pulled the tray back further and saw the hands, clasped above the stomach. The frozen cleavage above the dress, and the face, with the hair stiff and forever parted. The eyes closed with the white hoarfrost on the lids and lashes. I bent down and put my lips to the edge of hers. They felt like cold, abandoned plastic.

Let me go, I whispered.

Though it felt absurd, because there was nothing here that could clutch. There was nothing that could hear, there was nothing that could answer.

Then I heard a polite cough behind me.

Must go now, she said.

I must, I agreed. I raised my head and pushed the tray back into place. I heard the metallic scrape for the second time.

You find what you want? Clues?

There are no clues, I told her. Just a girl who threw herself in the river.

And there are too many of those, she said.

She jerked her head towards the corridor outside. She seemed to find my presence there amusing.

Surely one is too many, I said.

Yes, she said. I must remind myself never to do it.

39

I felt the need for an hour of Gertrude. Her scrabbling dog, her electronic cigarettes, her wheatgrass and her crème de menthe. She was mixing it in a blender with ice, into a pale-green-coloured smoothie, and she asked me if I wanted some. I shook my head and asked for water.

You should try these, she said, as she puffed on her tubular thing, works wonders for the nicotine crave.

I don't smoke, I told her.

Or only other people's. And only lately.

And I had smoked, I remembered, that morning, by the ambulance bay.

Tell me about the dead, I asked her.

I know nothing about them. I am fake, like I told your colleague, charlatan.

My wife, I began.

Ah, she said, you still have one? Things are looking optromistic.

Optimistic, I corrected her.

Yes, she said. Look on the bright side. The dead can't.

She is working on a dig, I said. She's uncovered a body, from centuries ago. It's causing riots.

Maybe it has unfinished business, and she exhaled a billow of smoke. She must have known how mysterious it made her. Those painted lips, those Slavic cheekbones.

Don't you get it, you damn rationista?

What's a rationista? I asked her.

You are. With that English thing you call logic. The dead can cause more trouble than the living. In fact, they invariably do.

How?

That business. Unfinished. They want us to finish it for them.

She inhaled some more and drank the green stuff. How do you think I make my living?

You just said you were a charlatan.

Doesn't stop the requests. The need. The palm read, the ouija board. All the best psychics are charlatans. It just depends, she said and smiled, how good a charlatan you can be.

She took a pack of cards and began to shuffle them, expertly.

I used to be a croupier. Same thing.

Where? I asked her.

Monte Carlo, she said. So, you want to play blackjack now or you want your cards read?

Neither, I said. I just wanted to talk.

You went to see her again, she said quietly. With the parents. And don't ask me how I knew. It is that English thing, logic. Deduction. Is your job.

I said nothing. And her eyebrows arched.

And? she said. Tell me, Jonathan.

My daughter talks about her.

Ahhh. So that's why Jonathan is here.

She hears her playing cello.

The way my darling Jonathan did.

Maybe.

And that is — what is the word? Begins with F.

I think you mean fucked.

Fucked, she said. Interesting word.

An English word, I told her.

Not Latin? Not romance?

No, I said. Pure Anglo-Saxon.

The dog leapt suddenly, from an embroidered chair on to my lap.

How do I stop this? I asked her.

I can hear the pain there, Jonathan. Just tell yourself it's your imagination.

I can't.

Then finish that business, whatever it is.

I don't know what you mean.

The dead business. Otherwise they whisper, they murmur, they don't know they're dead.

40

We both realise, don't we, Sarah said, this place is about to blow apart?

A little like us?

She had turned on the television, next to the fridge. And I realised I'd never even noticed it was there. There were pictures of burning tyres, of black-masked youths in coastal cities, pulling up pavements.

I gave them two weeks' notice. From today.

Because of me? I asked.

It's becoming impossible, anyway. Every stone we move causes a crisis. I'm getting a little tired of police protection, riot shields.

They never worried her before, I thought. But every word was a potential crisis, at the moment. So I didn't say it.

So you're leaving? With Jenny?

I was hoping we might leave.

We meaning, all three of us?

That's what it used to mean. To me, anyway.

And then we both heard it. The first arpeggio of the prelude to the first cello suite.

Oh God, she said. Help me, help me. It's coming from her room.

It was perfectly, beautifully played. And as she shivered and I put my arms around her, I wondered how I could notice things like that. Then I realised. It wasn't a cello playing. It was a violin.

Let me go and look, I said.

I can't, she said. I can't move. I know I should. I should go and protect her, but my legs won't function.

Sit down, I whispered. And I wondered why I was whispering. But the beauty of the playing seemed to demand it.

I moved her towards a kitchen chair, as though she was a marionette. I could hear her breathing, soft and shallow, and thought she was about to faint. But she clutched at the table leg, so hard that the veins seemed to pop. And I let her go and walked slowly towards the music, and Jenny's half-open bedroom door.

I pushed the door open, slowly, and heard it creak. I remembered I had heard a door creak before, to just that piece of music. But this was in a higher register, soaring towards the heavens. I felt I had never heard such chilling perfection. And the door swung to, and I saw Jenny standing by her perfectly tidy bed, playing her child's violin.

She was poised, head to one side, her cheek indented by the chin rest. Her small fingers, which had hardly been able to form basic scales, glided over the tiny finger-board, and her bow coursed across the strings, like a professional.

I could only stand and listen until she had finished. I looked from Sarah to her and back again, both of them framed by the open doors.

Where did you learn that, love? I asked gently, when she had hit the last two high sustained notes.

She teaches me, she said, with that maddening simplicity of hers.

Who teaches you? I asked, rather redundantly.

You know who, Daddy, she said.

I took the violin from her hands, laid it on the bed with the bow and led her into the kitchen. Sarah stared at her as if she were a stranger, some kind of interloper into our domestic domain. But Jenny hardly noticed. She ran towards her in just that girlish way she had, and clambered up on to her knee.

Good morning, Mummy.

It's not morning, darling. It's the middle of the night.

Sorry. I woke up. I was practising.

Yes, I heard.

I have a new piece – she began and then stopped. Some childish instinct must have kept her from elaborating further. And I wondered at that strange intuition as I lifted her from her mother's lap.

I'll take you to bed, I said. Your mother needs to sleep. There, kiss her goodnight.

I leant her forwards, so her lips ended up on Sarah's cheek. Sarah's hand reached up to touch her hair. But she didn't turn, or say a word, as if she couldn't. Some questions can't be asked, I surmised. I brought my lips to the crown of Sarah's head, and realised, with a sickening lurch in my stomach, that Jenny and I both shared something that she didn't.

Will you make sure she sleeps well tonight? Sarah asked, in barely a whisper.

I told her I would. So we both slept together that night, in the small wooden bed with the flower-pot covers and the wooden swan that hung from the strings that came from the light bulb. She said nothing more about the incident, fell almost immediately asleep in my arms as my feet dangled over the floor at the other end. And it was only in the morning, when she woke, that she made mention of any of it.

I was woken by her hand, tapping my cheek.

What happened to her, Daddy? she asked, briskly curious, so early in the morning.

Who? I asked. I felt it was my duty to pretend ignorance, although I already knew.

Little Petra.

Her parents lost her, I said as delicately as possible, when she was very young.

Like Hansel and Gretel, she said.

No, I told her, and began lifting her out of bed. Hansel and Gretel were left in the forest, as far as I remember. Something to do with a nasty stepmother.

So how did they lose her?

Maybe they lost her to music, I said, very anxious to change the subject.

She heard the music playing one day, and she followed it.

Yes, I told her. Something like that.

In the forest. There was a prince playing, in a clearing.

Maybe, I said.

41

There was a prince, playing in a clearing. I imagined him wearing one of those Tyrolean hats we see in fairy tales, a feather sticking out from the brim, in a pair of high, thigh-length boots as he strode through the under-growth, sawing his bow. The large mossy trees echoed with the music, intermingling with the sound of the morning bird chorus. Tiny hamlets scattered around and one child is woken first by the unearthly melody. She walks out and follows and is lost for ever.

I was daydreaming. I was taken out of it by one word.

Haunted.

Haunted. The Viennese repeated it, sceptically twisting the end of his moustache.

We deal in objective realities here, he said.

You do?

I was surprised, to say the least. Buried memories, suppressed desire, hidden motivations, marital secrets. There was nothing objective about any of them.

Perhaps, he said tentatively, the stresses of your situation has led to a parallel fantasy in your daughter.

And how do you explain – her sudden virtuosity?

You said she had heard the tune, he told Sarah. You had been playing the Bach collection by—

Casals, she said wearily, Pablo Casals, as if he should have already known.

I've handed in my notice, she continued. I can't take this any longer.

This – disturbance—

The whole thing. Jenny. The demonstrations, the riots, the sense of something just about to burst. The heat. And there's something my husband is not telling me.

I'm sure there is. That is the purpose of these sessions.

Maybe he can tell you. Can you tell him, Jonathan? Whatever is the hidden key, the secret, the unmentionable thing? Because we're leaving without you if you don't.

He waited, expectantly, but without any hope of illumination. As if he was too used to these scenarios to be really surprised.

She died, I said.

We already know that, Sarah almost spat. You left her the note and the next thing they pulled her from the river.

No, I said. She died before that.

Oh God, Sarah moaned, please take me out of here.

She died the night I met her, I said bluntly, coldly, as if none of it mattered any more.

Help me, doctor, Sarah said, this is the father of my child talking. This was a rational man, a functioning partner, a good parent.

I met a girl on the bridge. I pulled her from the water. I took her back to her apartment, on the other side of the river. When I traced a missing girl to the morgue in the twelfth district, it was her. And the records show that she died that night.

Isn't there a word for that, doctor? Insanity? Or perhaps necrophilia? He gets emotionally entangled with someone who's dead? At least his wife chose the living.

Please, Sarah—

There is no 'please' about it. I'm taking Jenny back to London. And I would like you to come, if you can rid yourself of this . . . thing – this obsession – this mad fucking—

And she stood.

I'm sorry, doctor. I have to go now.

After she'd left, we sat in silence for a while. I heard a street musician outside, playing through the opened window. I thought of the prince again, and his melody weaving through the mossy trees, like blowing hair.

You find it hard, the therapist said, and I understand, we all do. Something happened that you can't explain; it's like life, we can't explain the bulk of it, and though it's my job to pretend to, I know at heart I am – what is that word? – a charlatan.

That word again. I would have stopped him there, but he had some burning need to continue.

Take things at their face value, as they happen to you; you are presented with a puzzle and if there is a solution, find it. Does it matter if the elements of the puzzle are rational or irrational, happened to the individual or didn't happen? The result is the same. The problem is the same.

The trauma is the same. Who am I to say that the source of any upset is imaginary? I can see the result, the pathology in front of me. Whatever caused that gave rise to a physical outcome. So if imaginary causes lead to actual outcomes, can the cause be justifiably termed unreal, imaginary? No. It has its own reality. Its own rules. And if those rules can be found, be identified, be traced, then maybe a solution is possible.

He looked at me, his grey eyes burdened with some kind of inner exhaustion.

And I, like your wife, am tired of all of this. You are a detective – no? – of kinds. Your job is solutions. Not mine. My job is consolation. Of whatever kind I can offer.

42

There seemed only one place to go, under such histrionic circumstances. To the opera.

The large, over-decorated doors were locked. There was a cardboard sign, askew behind a glass window frame, and from the operatic sounds booming from the interior, I presumed what it said was that rehearsals were in progress. So I walked round, beneath the carved-stone caryatids, until I found a side entrance open.

I relished the gloom for a moment, as the voices echoed above me and the orchestra dutifully echoed them back. It was Verdi, I could tell, from the simple, almost peasant force of the melodies. Bo ba bo bo bo ba bum.

I climbed a narrow staircase which I assumed would lead me backstage, or somewhere close to the orchestra pit. But the steps just kept going, winding their way up into the impenetrable shadows above. There was a thin wintry sense of light then, and I saw a door and pushed it open, and found myself in a box, six seats covered in that tired dusty velvet and an equally red velvet balustrade.

There was a full rehearsal in progress on the stage, a chorus dressed in military fatigues and black ski masks and those that I could only assume were the principals dressed in the pastel-coloured balaclavas of the street riots. There was a set of crumbling Soviet-style buildings, strewn about with overturned monumental sculptures of muscular bronze workers, hammers and Kalashnikovs jutting from the stage rubble at unlikely angles. It was *Rigoletto*, in some post-modern interpretation, I could only presume, from the choruses that filled the empty auditorium; from the baritone, bent double far below me, moving like a crab through the apocalyptic wreckage of the set. I took a seat by the balustrade and bent my body like his, my chin against the velvet armrests, worn smooth by innumerable elbows, and listened to the small orchestra in the pit down there until the last aria had ended and a soprano dressed in pastel colours died in a black-clad figure's arms. Gilda, I assumed, the cursed one, remembering the conversation that could never have happened, in that same orchestra pit.

A director walked on from the wings and dismissed all of the cast but the hunchbacked baritone, who repeated an aria until his back seemed to trouble him, then sang it one last time, half upright. There were raised voices, a balaclava pulled off, and a plastic machine gun kicked across the boards. Differences of interpretation, I assumed, until the stage finally emptied and the orchestra began to pack.

I saw the first cellist rise and recognised from above his thinning hair, his shining patent-leather shoes as they stepped from the pit through the empty auditorium. Then they stopped, in a band of sunlight that lit the frayed carpet from the high windows and I thought for a moment he was about to bend down and polish them. But he didn't.

He looked up from his shoes, directly at me. He put one hand in his pocket, searching for something. Then he dropped his gaze and walked on, out of sight.

I sat there in the shadows as the orchestra cleared. I could hear the snap of music cases and the shuffle of departing players and the sound of a pair of shoes, mounting the stairs behind me. They were hard-heeled shoes of patent leather, I imagined. But I couldn't have been sure.

Then the door slowly opened, and it was him, all right, with an unlit cheroot between his lips.

You like opera? he asked.

I know very little about it.

You must like it, he said, to find your way up here.

Rigoletto, I muttered, and didn't know how to continue. I will admit to being curious.

Rigoletto, he said, was set in Mantua. Not in some post-Gorbachev wasteland. It can only cause trouble.

The balaclavas?

The whole thing. How do you say? The concept. Is difficult, he said, to play the cello solo with a riot in the auditorium. Enough of metaphor, I say. Just tell the story.

He took a plastic lighter from his pocket and struck it. I remember it was coloured green. The warm light lit his face from underneath.

So what is the story? I asked him.

As absurd as any opera. A hunchback. A daughter. A duke. A secret assignation. A curse.

He lit the small cigar, finally.

You should never have been there, he said then.

You knew, didn't you?

221

Tell me what I know.

That she was dead.

No. Not at first. I allowed myself some frisson of jealousy. Before I realised she had to be.

He blew the cigar smoke through his lips.

No smoking here, he said. But the place will be empty soon. Musicians make an exit quicker than hares, through the hatch. The minute they hear the bell.

He flicked the green-coloured lighter again. His face flared in the amber, and he seemed to relish the theatricality of the underlight.

That was our place, you see. Lovers have to have a place, don't they? A secret place. And not only in opera librettos. A bare mattress on a floor. A sink. Or a washbasin. If you are blessed, a bath or a shower. And we were blessed, for a while.

His eyes met mine and I looked away.

Why do you care? he asked.

Does it matter?

Yes. I sense a frisson of jealousy there too. But I have to admit I am puzzled. You act as if you knew her.

I imagine I do.

So tell me then. She was pulled from the river? Three or four weeks ago?

She was.

I suspected as much.

Why?

When things began to happen. My daughter heard music. You have a daughter? Of course. Of course. So maybe she hears it as well. Bach's cello suites. The D minor was her favourite. I taught her cello, if you must know.

She played at the orchestra?

No, he said. She never had that kind of talent. Too much vibrato. But she would have loved to. To sit beside me, as my second cellist, and play the Cortigiani solo. Would have been her dream. And she had many of those.

He tapped ash into his hand and crumbled it to nothingness.

I had an affair with my pupil. The worst of clichés, I suppose. In that apartment, where I would see you coming and going. And you want the whole story, of course you do. She would sit on that couch after – what do you call it – the thing, the event – and play her cello while I smoked in the other room. She had too much *expressivo*, too little restraint. But she had talent, I can't deny that.

He placed the cigar between his thin lips and drew once more.

And you, he said, what's your excuse? For haunting that place that was ours?

I was asked to find a girl, I told him, who had gone missing as a child.

And you tracked her to there? That little apartment? I would love to know how?

His eyes met mine once more. Small, brown. I would have described them as repellent.

You must like the damaged ones.

Pardon me?

He smiled, wistfully.

She had that extraordinary need, you see, for contact, that only comes from the damaged ones. And they can be exquisite, the damaged ones.

I don't understand, I said.

But I understood too well. Something broke inside me. It was his tone. The assumption of complicity.

Have you found that, in your life? No? You are English, of course. You mightn't know of such things.

I could have flung him over the balcony, down to the seats below. I imagined the crunch as his head hit the aisle.

I am good, he said, very good at keeping secrets. So you must have been good too? At searching them out? I met her on that bridge, if you must know. She was playing the cello, busking for coins. She made almost a living from it, from the passers-by, the tourists. It at least paid for that apartment where the lessons began. I would help with the rent there, after a time. And I wonder who pays for it now?

He looked puzzled for a moment. And I took a breath to calm myself.

Did she ever talk about her childhood?

Sometimes about nothing else. But the stories, they often changed. Two Romany musicians who started her playing in the metro. A father, who taught her violin. By ear.

She was taken, I told him, as a child.

Taken? By gypsies, like in a fairy tale? Who told you that?

Her parents. They hired me to find her.

Who hired you? The mother?

And the father.

How strange.

Why is it strange?

Because she wasn't taken. She ran.

Ran? From whom?

From him, who else? That village fiddler. So she told me.

I remembered his feet, rubbing spittle into my office carpet. His hands, like stolid blocks on his knees. And did all of the pieces fall into place then? No, they didn't. But I understood something, at last.

But who knows, maybe that memory was as unreliable as her . . . vibrato . . .

He narrowed his eyes.

She loved it and hated it. But she couldn't live without it.

Without what?

Music. Have you ever been terrified by music?

My wife has. Only last night.

Bach's cello suites. The serene heart of baroque. Has terrified my daughter. My household. My window broke the other night. Of its own accord. Perhaps I deserved it.

He raised one gleaming black shoe and stubbed the cigar out on the heel.

She told me she was pregnant, you see. I assumed it was another fantasy. She asked to meet me where I'd met her first. By that bridge. But I never turned up.

He blew air between his teeth.

Would you have? Yes, you probably would.

I did, I said. Some time later.

He whistled, for a moment. The first arpeggio.

And now it terrifies you. Well, he said, finally, perhaps you deserve it too.

He took an intake of breath through his thin nostrils. They seemed pinched, by invisible fingers.

Whatever the case, you are welcome to it.

He bowed his head slightly with odd formality, and seemed to click his heels. He turned towards the door, where he heard it.

A series of triplets, with one note ascending.

I thought the orchestra had left.

The bow now picked out a melody. Like a country dance.

They have, I told him. Like hares out of the trap.

Can you hear it?

I recognised the sixth cello suite.

Is there someone in the pit?

I glanced backwards. There was no one in the pit.

So, you have it on your phone, he said. A ringtone?

He took two steps down towards me and gripped my lapels, feeling for a phone. But it was silent, in my inside pocket.

So, he whispered, his face close to mine. She still plays for us. The D major suite. A cool, verdant key.

I pushed both hands away.

For us?

Or should I be jealous? he asked. He rubbed one hand off the other, as if to cleanse them.

For you.

And there was only an echo of the sound now.

Again, too much vibrato. But she is no longer my concern.

He bowed his head and stepped backwards towards the door.

She is – how do you say it? – all yours.

He turned and left the door swinging gently on its hinges. The sound reminded me of something. And as his feet down the steps retreated into silence and the door creaked on, I remembered.

The sign outside his house, *Musikinstrumente*, the slight wind blowing, the wood creaking against the metal.

43

The door I had entered was locked, so I climbed the side steps to the stage, over the orchestra pit where she had imagined she would one day play, where she had taken the pearls that had started all the trouble. Or had I imagined that, too? It was easy to imagine things, on that sloping stage with the crimson seats fanning out behind me and the dim gold-trimmed boxes above them. There could have been generations of ghosts here. Operatic ghosts: drowning Rhinemaidens and lost Eurydices and consumptive bohemian girls. I picked my way through the theatrical wreckage, over the plastic Kalashnikovs and the coloured balaclavas, to the wasteworld of ropes and pulleys and old scenic backdrops behind. I found a door there that would have led to a back- or side-street, and pushed the bar on it, prodded it open. The wave of late-summer heat struck me, but I was cold inside it. There was a tobacconist, pulling down the shutters over the window of his narrow little shop. I closed the door behind me and was walking down the metal steps when my phone rang.

You're late, Sarah said. She'll be waiting. And I can't believe you'd be late for her at a time like this.

Wasn't it your turn? I said.

No, she said, it was yours.

I shut off the phone and I ran. In a daze, or a panic, across the boulevard.

There was no one waiting for me on those wide steps when I reached them. A few students walking down them, with their music cases. There was the sound of a loud flute, playing the same phrase repeatedly, like someone's favourite ringtone. I ran up the steps, through the doors, into the dark interior, and the sweat was running down my hands. There were two broad staircases on either side of the wall, with high churchlike windows. The evening sun was pouring through them, catching dust and wheeling midges in the yellow light. I took the stairs two at a time, and had reached the balcony above before I heard it.

The series of triplets, with one note ascending. Played on a violin.

I turned. There was a dim corridor, with doors on the left-hand side. A series of benches. Two young girls sitting on them, their violin cases between their knees.

The melody then, like a country dance.

I followed it to an open door.

Jenny was standing in a dusty room, her small head cocked to one side, playing the sixth cello suite, in the cool verdant key of D major.

Her teacher turned to me and blinked, her eyes huge behind her glasses.

You've paid for extra lessons?

I said nothing.

Money well spent, she said. She has positively—

She stood then. Took the bow from Jenny's hand.

. . . leapt ahead. This new teacher is quite remarkable.

She opened Jenny's case, placed the bow inside it.

It sometimes happens. A pupil makes the old teacher redundant.

She grimaced slightly. Took off her glasses. Wiped her eyes.

Stick with the new one, then, I would say.

She took the violin from Jenny's chin. Placed it inside and closed the case over.

It has been a pleasure, thus far. I will leave her in the hands of – what is her name, dear?

Petra, Jenny said.

Petra, she repeated. I would have thought the cello suites were too advanced for these tiny hands.

And she took Jenny's hands in her own. The veins stood out above the bones.

But we have heard the evidence. I would have been wrong.

44

We took the metro back. It was crowded with the rush hour, so she sat on my knees on one single hard bench.

Your teacher was impressed, I whispered, into the curled hair around her ear.

Yes, she said. I'm coming on in leaps and bounds.

But you can't stop the lessons, I said.

Why not? she murmured. I have a better teacher now.

Jenny, I said, and turned her face towards me. You know none of this is real.

Isn't it? she asked.

I rubbed my finger on her lip.

It doesn't matter, she said. What matters is the music.

Do me a favour then, I asked. Give the music a break, for just one night.

Why?

Because. Sometimes it's good to take a break.

And it upsets Mummy, she said.

Are you reading my mind?

Maybe, she said. And maybe Petra is as well.

The train swayed and a woman with an armful of onions pressed into me.

Try to forget about Petra.

I can't, she said. Can you?

But she left the violin in its case that night, which was some kind of relief. I cooked for all three of us and the chopping of onions and the grinding of pepper took my mind off cellos and operas. I tucked Jenny in her bed and read another chapter about the disogred giant with the tender heart.

We have to leave, I said to Sarah, when I came back into the kitchen. She was sitting by the old wood table with a glass of wine and another cigarette.

Whyever, she asked, when it's so peaceful here?

Do I have to count the reasons?

Riots, she said, at my dig. A child who talks to dead people. Are there more?

I've one case to settle, then I can close the office down.

Does it involve a drowned girl?

A funeral, I told her, that I have to attend.

Why?

I can't tell you why, Sarah.

Jonathan, who can't tell me why.

I was hired to find a girl. She's being buried tomorrow.

You're burying a girl. I'm exhuming one. Maybe we both should stop.

We will.

Tell me it will be better in London.

It will be, I promise.

Myrtle Drive. Wimbledon. You remember it?

Where your mother lives. Monkey-puzzle trees.

Maybe we can settle in Richmond.

Staines.

Clapham.

Blackheath.

Hackney.

Why are we reciting names?

Because it's fun, I said.

But I was remembering the pink-tracksuited madam, and her place-name recitals. Anya, with her track marks.

Do they still exist, she asked, those places?

Maybe not, I said. Maybe it's just us.

I could live with that, she said, and curled her hand around mine. Just us.

She drank too much wine that night and I had to help her to the bedroom. I held her steady by the French windows and took her clothes off, piece by piece. Her blouse first, with barely noticeable sweat stains under the arms. She turned, swaying, and I unclasped the bra, which she cupped, for a moment, in her elbows, like a bad schoolgirl. I unzipped her skirt and let it fall to the floor and had to hold her hand while she stepped beyond it. I lifted her then and carried her to the bed.

Do you remember, she asked me, how much fun it used to be?

Yes, I told her. I remember very well.

45

The train followed the river out of the city into the dull, parched countryside. I sat with Istvan in an empty carriage and tried to read the headlines of the newspaper he held in front of him.

You want news? he asked. Minister for State Security has resigned.

Why?

Because there is none. No state, no security. Riots all over. And because he was found with a rubber-suited woman above a tyre shop.

Vulcanizace, I pronounced, quite proudly.

Circus tricks, he said. Maybe onetime colleague Frank took the picture.

Maybe.

We should tout for business, he said, closing the paper. We should expand – how you say?

Our horizons, I ventured.

Yes, horizons. Soon there will be bodies all over. Security in high demand.

You do it, I said. I'll be leaving soon.

Wise, maybe.

You think?

You leave Istvan to expand horizons. Take your family back where?

London.

Wise. Very wise. So tell me why we travel to the arse end of nowhere to observe the funeral of the girl we were hired to find? We found her. Case closed.

Because her mother thanked me once.

For what?

For believing.

Are you religious, Jonathan?

Not particularly.

Superstitious. You believe in *psychiki*.

Only under duress.

Duress, he repeated. It was a new word to him.

And we never found out why.

Why what?

Why she left. All those years ago.

46

There was a small, beautifully sad station by a high grassy berm which hid the river. The train deposited us and moved off along those tracks which made two straight lines below the irregular blur of the berm and led deep into the steppes to a point beyond infinity.

It was a fortification, Istvan told me. Something to do with tank movements in the Second World War.

We walked, then. Through the station, where a set of broken eaves pointed towards a village beyond.

It was one of those circular medieval keeps, with some odd monastic history, with a dry moat running the circumference and a tributary of the river flowing behind. Scattered breezeblock bungalows lay on either side of the broken roadway and lent a melancholy modernist contrast to the pale, off-white limestone of the high walls, the dark, sloping roofs inside them.

There was a bell ringing, a mournful toll as we walked down the cracked pathway of dried mud, cigarette ends and scattered beer cans. For some reason, I thought of the road to Emmaus.

We are either early or late, Istvan said sagely.

We crossed a mound of earth that could have once been a drawbridge, through an old stone archway without gates.

Once, said Istvan, there were villages like this all over. Can you imagine?

I could. The ancient walls with the cracked limestone, the tiny ripples of something like streets, with misshapen doorways and small shuttered windows. I could imagine a young girl running down them, kicking back her heels.

There was a cone or a pyramid rising above the perimeter wall with an off-centre iron cross. That was the church, and there was a shuffle of people moving from it, hardly a procession, towards the archway opposite and the graveyard beyond.

A meandering ribbon of water flowed around it. It must have fed the allotments on the other side, the small communal gardens with their tangles of bean and tomato rows, with hooped coverings of plastic. There was an intermittent, ruined forest beyond, huge beeches and oaks separated by saplings. One could imagine Zhukov's tanks ploughing through it, years ago. And Putin's, doing the same, some day soon.

We stopped in the shadow of the other arch. It seemed impolite to go further. I could see the coffin under the shoulders of four men, in the fierce, punishing midday sun. An Orthodox priest walking before it, holding Petra's mother's arm. There was a mechanical digger by an open grave. And as they made their way towards it, I recognised the face that had spat on the office carpet, the shoes that had ground the spittle on the floor. He was the left-hand bearer, in a dark Sunday suit.

Why are we here? asked Istvan again.

Because here is where she ran from.

She didn't run. The mother told us, she was snatched.

No, I said. She ran.

Every kid runs from these places, he said. Sooner or later.

But she ran from him.

I nodded towards him, diminutive in his Sunday suit, bearing most of the weight of the coffin. His face glistened with sweat in the heat. They were at that awkward point at which they had to loose it from their shoulders. There was a flurry of movement from behind them, hands gripping, taking the burden. He stood back, released, and rubbed his shoulder, as if to ease the pain.

Ayee.

Istvan whistled through his browning teeth.

You have evidence?

The only evidence was dead now. So I shook my head.

It all makes sense.

So how does she find – what you call closure?

Like in the cable series?

And the coffin was being lowered now, on brown leather straps.

She is dead. Isn't that closure enough?

I suspect not.

In these kinds of places, peasant places, they manage things in their own country way.

Aren't there laws to deal with things like this?

No law out here. Soon no law anywhere.

But they don't know.

No, he said. Not yet.

He grimaced. I could have almost called it a smile.

You go back to station. Have a beer. Leave this to me.

I sat in the empty station as two trains passed. And the third was trundling by as Istvan joined me once more.

Come, he said. We can't afford to miss this.

So we took the train back, along the endless berm, until the river made its appearance behind it, glowing gold, like the molten Euphrates. He said nothing for a long, long time.

Then.

I spoke with the mother.

And?

She already suspected.

How?

She is a mother.

Was it why she hired us?

Perhaps. And now she knows. She has brothers and cousins who will ... how do you say it ... deal with the whole sad situation, in their own special way.

I had heard that phrase before. A baby-faced cleric, in a bouffant beard and turban. Kill them, he said, in your own special way.

And Jonathan—

He smiled, as if to change the subject.

Your name is dactyl, you know that?

Three syllables, I said. One long, two short.

She told me to tell you to do what she can't do.
And what is that?
Let go.
Let go, I repeated.
Sometimes there is no closure, Jonathan.

47

He drove me from the city station to the end of my street.

The first time, he said, I ever saw where you lived.

A suburban house, I told him, with Tyrolean pretensions.

The Tyrol, he said. Maybe some day I will visit. I think I might prefer London.

So might I, I said. And for some reason I gripped his arm.

So, Jonathan, he said. Is this goodbye?

No. Not yet, I said. Though I sensed it wasn't true. I was getting good at this half-truth business. I slid my hand down his forearm and did a strange thumbshake. And I realised how bad I was with manstuff.

As I approached that gate made of carved wooden gargoyles covered in roughly trowelled plaster I heard music playing again. Not the violin, this time, or the cello. But the lazily strummed guitar chords of Joni Mitchell. And I walked in to find Sarah cutting onions in the kitchen, an open bottle of wine beside her.

I'm hoping Joni has powers of exorcism, she told me. And that dead cellists don't like rock and roll.

I tried to kiss her, but she turned her head away. There were tears in her eyes – from the onion, I hoped.

You call that rock and roll? was my attempt at humour.

But it fell almost immediately flat. Because the violin began to play again from Jenny's room, in strange counterpoint. A gigue, or a gavotte, one of those baroque dances.

She's been playing on and off all evening, she said. She gets better every moment. Deceased teachers have a lot to recommend them, don't they? Maybe we could open a music school. The Academy of Dead Music. Or what is that old stuff called? Baroque?

I've booked flights, she said. If we get away from here, maybe it will all stop? Or will this thing persist at thirty thousand feet?

She turned up the Joni Mitchell to a deafening volume.

Never thought I'd miss it, she said. Those old three chords. And Joni's right. You don't know what you've got till it's gone. I used to think it was noise, just noise. The thumping beat, the repeated phrases, love me do, heart of glass, I want to be your dog. Iggy Pop now, he's the one to banish this shit, I saw him in the Marquee on Wardour Street when I was young and half a punk. Can you imagine me with my cropped hair and my pierced lip bouncing up and down in a slashed T-shirt to that divine skinny god pogoing on the stage? But I know what it was about now, Jonathan, it was about life, all that noise and that sweat and that spit, that chaos, that cacophony, the three chords and the voices you could hardly hear, it was about living, not this . . .

And I could hear the violin, above it all.

. . . this death . . .

Then she swept the onions to the floor.

Talk to her, Jonathan. Please make it stop.

So I left the Joni Mitchell playing and walked towards the door behind which a thin and perfect violin etched out a different world. I opened the door to see Jenny reaching the end of a gigue or a saraband or a gavotte.

I think Mummy doesn't like me playing, she said as she turned towards me. Maybe I should stop.

You should, love, I said. For the moment at least.

And there was something dangling from the wrist of her bow-hand. A string of pearls, delicate and black. Symbols of hope, I remembered the shop assistant had called them. Hope, for wounded hearts.

Where did you get those, darling? I asked in a voice so low it could hardly be heard over the raucous music from the kitchen.

But Jenny heard me.

Petra, she said. She gave them to me.

48

There will be no school tomorrow, I promised her, if you give those stones to me.

Pearls, she said, they are pearls.

Pearls, I repeated, and managed to slide them from her wrist.

And there was no school, next morning. The computers were down, the electricity intermittent. The net had slowed to something less than a crawl. Maybe anything other than the most basic forms of communication were suspect. The riots had spread on the web and were multiplying, like a self-nurturing virus. We couldn't print our boarding passes for the plane, and so drove into the city, taking Jenny with us. I had packed most of her things, and locked her violin under the full weight of her clothes. And there was a different kind of heat in the slow movement of traffic, something sultry in it, with a bank of cloud above the buildings that seemed as if it was waiting to burst.

London will be better, Sarah said from the back seat. Myrtle Drive, Wimbledon, and Granny Tilda.

Do I have to leave all of my friends? Jenny asked.

Only the imaginary ones, Sarah said.

That's almost funny, I told her, and caught her eye in the rear-view mirror.

Why is it funny? Jenny asked.

Because, Sarah said. Just because.

Because I have no other kind, Jenny said, and Sarah's thin smile vanished in the mirror.

Oh God, she said. Play some music. Some bad rock and roll.

So I found a station on the radio that played the kind of out-of-date rock they favoured there. Some strange time zone just after punk, around when the Wall fell. Milli Vanilli, the Fine Young Cannibals, Spandau Ballet, promising a future that seemed more past than the unmentionable baroque of Johann Sebastian Bach.

There were soldiers at street corners in full riot gear and I wondered what government departments could afford those knee-pads of Velcro, those stun grenades, those Heckler & Koch machine guns, those Kevlar vests.

I had the pearls in my pocket and played with them as I drove, like worry beads. And my main worry was that she would mention them to Sarah. But with that impeccable instinct of hers, all she talked of was the trip ahead of her.

I've been in planes before, she said, brightly.

Yes, said Sarah. Many times.

And we're going in a plane now because—

She held up her fingers, as if she was about to count the reasons.

Because of the trouble, darling, Sarah said. Because some things aren't safe here.

Because of my imaginary friends, she said.

Because your grandmother wants to see you.

Granny Tilda. Who lives in Myrtle Drive. In the house with the monkey-puzzle tree.

You remember it?

I remember the tree.

The bridge was blocked to traffic, so I parked the car on the east side. I looked back at the building behind me and saw a slash of yellow in the upper window. So I knew Gertrude was awake, probably drinking her wheatgrass smoothie. I walked them both across the bridge then, and Jenny held my hand tight, as if she was afraid to let go. There was a scattering of rubbish on the bridge: broken glass, a twisted bicycle tyre, and the remains of what looked like gas canisters. But some things never changed. Groups of forlorn tourists took pictures of themselves with the river as a backdrop, and I noticed police barges, churning up the brown water. On the other side, the traffic was flowing and the streets seemed to have assumed some semblance of normality.

I led them towards the half-finished mall that housed the travel agent's and told them I would meet them by the corner there, in one hour's time.

Come with us, Jenny said.

He can't, darling. He has an office to close up.

You have a meeting, Daddy, Jenny said brightly.

Yes, I told her. I have a meeting.

Then Jenny suddenly, and unaccountably, smiled.

What's so funny? I asked.

Look, Mummy.

What?

Daddy's trousers.

I was standing on a grating. There was a hot wind, blowing upwards from it, making balloons of my trouser-legs. I thought of the giant blow-dryer of the river god and stepped backwards, as if burnt.

An hour, said Sarah.

Don't be late.

49

She held the pearls in her hand as the dog made scraping sounds around the parquet floor.

She can walk now, I said, to fill the silence.

Yes, said Gertrude, patella is fine. But there will be other reasons to keep her housebound.

So it is time to leave?

How do you say it? High time.

The pearls seemed to glow blacker in her pale, manicured hand.

You bought these?

In the jeweller's, by the opera house.

But they went on a dance then. Like in that play by Schnitzler.

What play?

La Ronde. Someone should make an opera of it.

I would like you to have them.

Why me? she asked.

Because, I said, they would suit you.

So they will end their travels here? In this old hand.

Elegant hand.

Nice try, Jonathan. It was elegant once.

So you can keep them for me.

Keep them for you? If you ever return?

Something like that.

Among my other souvenirs.

She held them towards the window and turned them in the band of sunlight coming through it.

Black pearls, she said. Be still, my heart.

They can't hurt you.

Can they hurt, these pearls?

Others, maybe. Not you.

Is there something you're not telling me now?

Too many things.

I closed her hand around them.

Please, I asked. Take them. Do me one last favour.

She smiled then, and raised her face towards mine.

I can take them, Jonathan, she said. But don't think it will help.

Help what? I asked, rather stupidly.

She's not attached to these. She's attached to you.

I looked at her face, in that band of sunlight. It was unkind to her. The lines showed beneath the impeccable make-up. She looked for once like what she said she was. A retired croupier. Or a charlatan. Somewhere beyond, I heard a siren wail.

But I'll hold them for you.

I kissed her, on the corner of her pencilled lips.

Goodbye, Jo-na-than.

Would I hear those three syllables again, separated just like that? I wondered, as I made my way back across the river.

Some part of me hoped I wouldn't. And some part of me knew I would.

I walked to that grating, where what she had called the river god blew hot air from underneath. I waited there, feeling the hot wind fanning my hair upwards, but Sarah and Jenny didn't come. I heard the sounds of running feet then, all around me, but could see nothing moving on the street, and realised the sounds were coming from below.

It was a ventilator for a metro platform, the hot air was coming from the passing trains and I saw a mass of coloured balaclavas then, through the grating, surging towards some exit way beyond.

There was a metro entrance by the half-built mall and I could see police running towards it, blowing whistles, pulling guard sticks, black vans screeching down the roadside, more police spilling out of the opening doors and the pastel-coloured mob trying to burst through, and I saw Sarah hurrying towards me, her arm around our daughter, as the mayhem spread about behind them. Then Jenny broke free of her and ran into my arms.

Mummy bought me sandals, Daddy, she said.

Just get us out of here, said Sarah, so I took one hand of Jenny's as Sarah took the other and we hurried towards the river, half-swinging her between us.

Pretend it's a game, Sarah said, so I pretended, and swung her, with those coloured canvas plimsolls, across the wide empty road to the parapet on the other side.

There was a thundering sound then, of a hundred running feet to my left, and I took her in my arms and pressed her body into the granite steps cut into the parapet wall and something hit me, a placard or a riot shield, and I fell and could see Jenny's coloured sandals against the blue sky beyond through the wave of running figures like bright coloured hummingbirds in Doc Marten boots. I could see Sarah, pressed against the granite wall, and was trying to rise when they swarmed all around me in their coloured balaclavas and I was pushed to the ground and lost sight of them both. All I could see were the black-camouflaged ones and after them the Kelvar-suited military police. There was a chaos of boots, all of the same colour, rounding on the bridge, and I could see the real encounter happening there, the pastel-coloured dervishes running past the giant hawsers, underneath the monumental angels where they were trapped, by a phalanx of black ski masks coming from the other side.

I heard a scream of loss, of hysteria, of pure unbridled terror. I hoped it was coming from the bridge. But when I got to my feet I realised it wasn't. It was coming from Sarah.

She was leaning over the parapet, like a drunk about to vomit. I pulled her back. I had seen what she had seen. A pair of coloured sandals, kicking in the brown water below. I jumped on to the parapet, and for the second time I dived.

I hit the river badly and thought for a moment my back had broken. But I managed to turn in the soupy murk and could see a figure above me, arms spread-eagled, face down, the sunlight pouring all around her in fingers of amber. I flailed up towards it and managed to turn her body when I broke the surface.

I could see that she was breathing, and called out her name.

She spewed water from her mouth. She took a gulp of clear air.

Jenny.

She managed a word. It sounded like yes.

Hold me.

I'm saying goodbye, she said, with another huge inhale. To the river.

Put your arms around my neck.

I'm saying goodbye to her.

Hush.

But she doesn't want us to go.

Please, love. Please. Don't talk. Hold me.

I could hear the deep-throated rumble of police barges moving towards us. I could hear distant screams from the bridge. And I could see those pastel-coloured, vainly flailing figures subsumed in wave after wave of black.

50

The summer saved us in the end. The warm, fetid water. They wrapped us in those silver blankets when they had pulled us to the barge, but they were quite unnecessary in that punishing heat. They sprayed us down with disinfectant and there was time to wonder, as the barge passed beneath the bridge, if they would afford the same courtesy to the ones being bruised and broken above us.

Sarah was waiting on the jetty. She almost crushed her daughter in her arms, burying her face into the crinkled silver.

I saw her, Mummy, she said.

Please, love, please.

She's down there and she doesn't want us to go.

Dear Jesus.

It's OK, I told her, it's OK.

No it's not OK, she said. It will be OK when we get out of here.

An ambulance took us home, one more siren to add to the general wail.

You two have to go, I whispered. Let me follow on later.

Why? she asked.

I think you know why, I said.

And she said nothing, so I assumed she did.

And when the taxi came to take them off it was night
again, and raining, one of those tropical summer downpours. I used that silver heat blanket as a kind of covering
tent when I carried their bags out to the car. Sarah lifted
Jenny to my face to give me a goodbye kiss and she asked
for it seemed the hundredth time why I couldn't come.
Because he has to settle things up, her mother told her, he
has to pack the rest of our belongings.

The rain was coursing through the porch roof in contin-
uous drips and she raised her face to it to say goodbye to
all of her non-existent friends. And to one in particular
that she assumed was crying.

She doesn't want us to go, she told her mother, and
Sarah replied that the friend had me to keep company
with.

What do you mean, Jenny asked, isn't he coming soon?

Yes, but not now.

Why not now? she asked again, and Sarah had to lift her,
almost drag her to the car, saying, Because he's tainted,
that's why, because he's haunted.

It was an odd word, I thought, watching the car vanish
into that silvery downpour. It was they who were like
ghosts, slipping quietly into another world. I was stuck
here, in the real world, with the rain falling and the sun
coming up tomorrow in that house through which the
water coursed now, like a miniature river. The imagination
was my element and I would live in it now, until they were

safe and well out of this slippery morass. But I stood there for a long time under the dripping porch and watched the laurel and linden trees create their own umbrella'd waterfalls. The road outside turned into a small river and whatever cars made their way down it threw up solid walls of spray. Then even the cars stopped and there was just the continuing rain.

After an hour or so I walked inside, where the water was covering the carpet. I could have closed every door but I didn't, I couldn't be bothered, because part of me welcomed this biblical flood. I turned on the television that had been hidden all this time, tucked beside the fridge, and sat on a wooden chair and propped my feet against the kitchen table. The news flickered away there, mutely, and from what I could gather the riots had flared up spontaneously, savagely, and were on the cusp of general anarchy when the rains took over. A revolution cannot compete with a downpour. On the news station anyway, as the handheld footage of youths in hoods and balaclavas being beaten by black truncheons gradually gave way to flooded vistas, the river spilling its banks, poplar trees looming like pencils out of mirrored fields, cars turning sideways as the floods engulfed them.

They were well out of it, I thought again and began to wonder about the dimensions an aeroplane occupies, how it collapses space and time and makes nonsense of the weather. They would be sitting now, one head resting on the other's shoulder, in a turbulent tube at thirty thousand feet. How real could that be? I wondered, yet real it absolutely was, as real as the mice struggling through the water beneath me, their underground tunnels flooded, their homes a watery grave. Were they mice, even? They could have been voles, if voles ever made their homes beneath the floorboards. And I must have sloshed across the kitchen floor to grab the one remaining whisky bottle, because it sat beside me on the table now, together with a glass, no ice. And I wondered how those chimney turrets were doing in the downpour; would the Tyrolean roof survive? It seemed designed to withstand storms of snow, not rain. And after a while the footage of the floods exhausted even the television screen, because it reduced itself to a small white dot, and then a half-grey, flickering haze.

I walked into the bedroom and found it had fared better than the kitchen and the hallway. The French windows were closed and all I could see through them was the haze caused by the never-ending rain. And I fell asleep to the sound of it and it must have been comforting enough, because the sleep was comparatively dreamless.

I spent four or five days in that house. It would have been impossible to leave, even if I'd wanted to. When the electricity failed, I played the Casals CDs on Jenny's coloured little boombox. So I had a cello to go with the sound of falling water. And when the dampened batteries on that gave out, I imagined the sound. I imagined a cello I could crawl into; it sat in the hallway like an enormous, malignant cat. The S-shaped curve beneath the strings allowed me in and I curled up there, on the sofa, and the strings vibrated with the magnificent sound, but there was too much vibrato, too much emotion in the playing. There was a coloured canvas shoe to distract me from it, and the instep of the foot beneath it and the whisper of released clothing and the breath of the refrigerated tray with the stiff body on it and the frozen eyelashes and the birthmark on the underside of the knee, like an *unde*, a dove, that flew away across the biblical flood.

I imagined the dove flying high above the city, the city sinking into the river until the river became a lake, and the lake and the sky above became one. And all that was left were those cello suites, a blur of blue, a blur of grey and a thin indeterminate line in between. And the rains must have stopped then, because I was in the kitchen, eating the peas from a once-frozen bag, when I heard a sound behind me. The sound of feet, wading through the stilled pond beneath the porch.

This is a mess, she said.

I turned, and saw that it was Gertrude, dressed in a light rain mac and a pair of wellington boots. She was perfectly reflected in the water beneath her.

I would say so, I replied.

You live in a pond. No one can live in a pond.

Doesn't the whole city now? Live in a pond of sorts?

Most of us have ways of coping. Sandbags, rescue services, water pumps. But you, Jonathan, have become . . . how do you say . . . a spermatozoa . . .

In the amniotic fluid of something or other.

Doesn't matter, Jo-na-than. You are not a newt or a water creature. You are a detective, of sorts.

I was, indeed I was.

You want your life back?

I looked at her and smiled, and shrugged. She looked absurd, in that rain mac and those wellington boots. She needed another context. Not this watery one.

I had a thought, she said. You stopped on that bridge to talk to her.

Is the bridge still there?

Of course the bridge is still there. Whole city is still there. It will recover.

That's good.

But my point is, Jonathan, anyone else could have done the same.

She took her hand out of her pocket, and I saw the pearls. The black ones. She stood by the submerged kitchen lintel and held them out so they were reflected in the kitchen floor.

You could pass her on, she said.

To whom? I asked.

To another. This attachment. Could replicate itself. Is – how you say it? – a pathology anyway . . . that you must be rid of . . .

And how would I achieve that?

If you know someone who deserves it. You effect some introduction. In the old-fashioned way.

51

There were damp sandbags in every doorway, there were municipal workers with unnaturally wide brushes pushing small tsunamis of brown water in front of them. There were whirlpools around every drain, but the traffic was flowing once more. I had dried the battery on my phone and called Frank, and told him he was indeed right, we should sit down and have a proper talk. So we met in a café and talked, me in my dampened suit, he in a kind of camouflage outfit, with military boots and a black ski mask tucked into the shoulder-band. He had changed, I mentioned, briefly, by way of a greeting. Everyone has changed, he said. You have seen the news? I had, I told him, and assumed he wasn't talking about the water. No, he said, and adjusted the cuffs on his well-pressed khaki shirt and I saw that he was still wearing cufflinks. So we should talk, he said, and we began.

We talked about everything but the matter in question, about the riots, the rains, until eventually, when the coffee was cold, he asked me, in the way of men who are used to dealing with the world, to come to the point.

I have to stop blaming her, I told him. Much of the fault was mine. When fissures like this erupt between couples, both parties have issues to deal with and must take their share of the blame. Do I detect a whiff of the therapeutic couch? he asked me, smiling. There's no couch involved, I told him, and it's not like that, not like the cliché at all, it's more a conversation with oneself, but sadly, the kind of conversation one cannot have with oneself, only through another. So the other is the conduit, he said. Yes, I agreed, to the kinds of realisations one should make on one's own, but rarely can. Are we talking forgiveness here? he asked. Yes, we are, I said, but I also know how little there is to forgive. The difficulty, I told him, is forgiving oneself.

But.

But, he said. There would have to be a but.

Yes. But. I would ask you for a favour. I need a gift returned.

To a woman? he asked.

Yes, to a woman.

So I can allow myself the satisfaction of being right, he said. There was a girl.

There was a girl.

And you would like me to deal with her.

Yes.

As a – what is the Latin? Quid pro pro.

Something like that.

Tell her what? That your marriage goes on? You can't see her again?

All of that.

Give her a shoulder to cry on? Because ...

Because you're that kind of man.

That women like to spill their hearts out to.

Sometimes more than their hearts.

We can't help who we are.

No. And give her this.

I wound the bracelet of black pearls round my fingers. They reflected the café we sat in, the stained-glass windows, the curved ceiling, in their dark uneven way.

It will mean a lot to her?

Yes, I said. And to me.

We crossed the bridge then. The river was swollen like a fat worm that had fed too much on a bloated corpse. The humidity had come back wholesale and I was sweating in my already damp suit. He seemed immaculate, though, walking beside me and talked about tides of history that were coming this way, how the neutered, degendered flowers of the west could never thrive in that hard ancient Slavic soil. Were these new opinions, I asked him, or did he always think that way, trying to imagine Sarah listening to such bilge, but no, he told me, much like my therapeutic experience, it was a matter of uncovering a layer of thought he always knew was there. There are times, he told me, where one has to think straight.

Nail one's colours to the mast.

I offered him the cliché for nothing.

Yes, he said. Otherwise the future won't be black or white, will be a . . .

He was searching for a word.

A rainbow, I offered again.

No, he said. A mess. A pastel mess.

We made our way then through the cobbled streets I hadn't seen for a while, and I was sad to see that most of the cobbles had been lost, ruptured, torn out of their sittings by the floods. They were being piled in untidy pyramids now by municipal workers. But I heard it then, the sound I hadn't heard for a while, and he must have heard it too, because he asked me, Did she play the cello?

She did, I said, and we could see the tiled arch now, the miraculous sound coming from above or inside it.

Can you hear that? I asked him.

Of course, he said. Bach. The second suite, in D minor.

I was mildly surprised at his erudition.

We know our music here.

We walked inside the arch. And he was right. Of course, they knew their music.

The courtyard was a mess of sandbags and sad grey pools that reflected the grey sky above. But the melody soared above it, which time or tide could never mess with.

And you want me to give her this?

The black pearls were in his hand. And I realised, for the first time, that they weren't black at all. They were a delicate dove-grey.

Just follow the sound, I told him. Up those steps. And be nice to her.

What else would I be? he murmured. And I did wonder what else, as he walked up the fan of dark concrete steps and was soon out of sight.

52

Am I a charlatan, Jonathan? she asked me at the departure terminal. She was that kind of woman: she liked goodbyes, at bus stops and metro platforms, train stations and airports.

No, I told her, you're a croupier and card reader and the best of friends.

There was a crush of panic around the security gates, with every conceivable form of luggage: bulging plastic sacks, cases wrapped in twine, army-surplus bags. Three-generation families, dark Roma hair, babies in papoose scarves.

Maybe I should go back, she said. To Monte Carlo. Wear a black necktie and a formal waistcoat and a very short skirt.

It might be better than here. But, I told her, they have casinos in London.

London?

And in Brighton. And in Blackpool. And probably in Weston-super-Mare.

London, she said. *Séance on a Wet Afternoon.*

You liked that one?

That Richard was in it. Hard to pronounce.

Attenborough, I said.

Say hello to London, she said. And to your wife. A pity I never got to meet her. And you must kiss little Phoebe before you go.

I kissed her first. Her make-up was perfect that evening, all of the lines masked in a film of foundation, the lips etched perfectly with the thin pencil, the eyes shaded with powder blue.

Then I kissed the Pomeranian, and lost myself in the gypsy crowd.

A NOTE ON THE AUTHOR

Neil Jordan was born in 1950 in Sligo. His first book of stories, *Night in Tunisia*, won the *Guardian* Fiction Prize in 1979, and his subsequent critically acclaimed novels include *The Past, Sunrise with Sea Monster, Shade* and *Mistaken*. The films he has written and directed have won multiple awards, including an Academy Award (*The Crying Game*), a Golden Bear at Venice (*Michael Collins*), a Silver Bear at Berlin (*The Butcher Boy*) and several BAFTAs (*Mona Lisa* and *The Crying Game*). He lives in Dublin.

neiljordan.com